Victims

by Amy Barkman

Victims

© 2018 by Amy Barkman

Published by Voice of Joy Publications

All Scripture quotations are from the King James Version.

Cover Design: Nick Delliskave

ISBN-13: 978-0998352060

ISBN-10: 0998352063

Dedication

To all the Victims in this fallen world – may the love of Jesus solve your problems, make you survivors, and give you joy!

Joy is sorrow overcome
Joy is love triumphant

Acknowledgements

As always, I couldn't do anything in the field of writing without the help of my daughter Ginny – author Virginia Smith. God bless you richly!

Thank you Tracy Ruckman for giving me back the rights to my novella so I could incorporate and expand it here.

Thank you again to Nick Delliskave for another wonderful book cover.

Thank you to Marie Garland for proofreading *Victims* and to her, Susie Smith, Jacque Lea, and Betsy Banks for your encouragement.

And especially thank You to Jesus for giving me parables to share.

Chapter One

The water slowly began to turn color but there was no one there to see it happen. It started at the deep end with a single stream of crimson which quickly dispersed. But the blood kept flowing, and flowing, and flowing. The surrounding area became tinged with pink. But by the time there was no more blood to pour forth, it had traveled throughout the thirty-six-foot-long pool and become invisible.

The smell of fresh coffee stirred her senses until her eyes finally opened. Susan Adams stretched and yawned when her feet hit the thick carpet of her bedroom floor. Stevie was so sweet, always leaving coffee to greet her when she awakened. She slipped her feet into house shoes and shuffled off to follow the scent. There was a card propped up beside the coffee pot. This one was musical and played "You Are My Sunshine" when opened.

She sat at the table, opening and closing the card as she sipped the hot beverage and felt the caffeine drive away the residual sleepiness from her mind.

Today what should she do? She grabbed the notebook and pen from their place in the square wooden bowl at the center of the table. She clicked the gel pen, placed it on the sheet of paper, and waited for the list to surface out of the fog in her brain.

By the time the coffee cup was empty, the page was filled with tasks to accomplish. Susan looked at the wall clock. Nine thirty. The pool would open at ten. But she had so much to do today, and swimming was not on her list.

At five 'til ten she pulled her BMW out of the driveway and headed toward town. The first thing on her list was the county library. It was one of her favorite places and today as always, she enjoyed browsing through the shelves, reading back covers, and choosing her fare for the next week.

When she returned to the car with the patron limit allowance of twelve books, she heard her cell phone ringing as it lay there on the passenger seat. She ignored it. There was way too much to do today to waste time talking on the phone.

Sheriff Jim Murray waited patiently while the Lee woman took in deep gulps of air and tried to stop the sobs that kept interrupting her account of finding the body. When she was able to continue, she nodded at him and he pulled the notebook out of his pocket.

"I came to unlock the gate at ten like I do every

morning. And today I planned to swim for a few minutes." Her eyes swept downward at the two-piece bathing suit she wore, but Jim purposefully did not let his eyes do the same. Although it was tempting. The bathing suit was very well filled.

Her eyes brimmed with tears again and her left hand flew up to her mouth. But the wailing didn't resume. This time he got her first name, Angie.

"I put my towel on that lounge chair." She indicated the brightly colored beach towel lying nearby. The cell phone she'd used to call for help lay beside it. "But just as I was about to dive in, I saw him."

"And you recognized him?"

"Oh yes!" She paused, and a hint of a smile touched her lips. "The bathing suit. Paul's famous in the neighborhood for that pair of trunks."

Jim looked over at the gurney where the paramedics placed the lifeless body. The tiger striped swim trunks were a brighter orange than any real tiger would sport.

"And Paul's full name?"

"Paul Adams. He lives right there." She turned to face the gate and pointed across the street.

"Family?"

She nodded. "Yes, his wife, Susan. They have a daughter, but she lives in California, an actress wannabe." The last phrase clearly conveyed disgust.

He looked across the street and took a deep breath. "I guess I'd better go tell Mrs. Adams about this." At age fifty-nine, he wasn't yet steeled against breaking bad news.

She shook her head. "She's not there. I live in the next block and she drove past my house just as I came out to walk down here."

He frowned. "Do you know any way we could reach her? Does she have a cell phone?"

"I have the number at my house. I'm not close to Susan, but I have everyone's information because I'm the secretary for the neighborhood association. And that's why I open the gate to the pool. It's part of my job."

The attendants were rolling the now covered body of Paul Adams out to the ambulance that was parked on the curb in front of the entrance. They would take the body immediately for an autopsy. The coroner followed close behind them and looked back over his shoulder at Jim. "I'll call as soon as I get the results."

Jim nodded and turned to Angie Lee. "You'd better lock back up now. Deputy Morales will stay here and secure the area until we can gather whatever evidence there may be."

He gestured for her to precede him through the gate. "I'll walk to your house with you unless you'd rather go in the squad car."

The look on her face was answer enough. No one wanted their neighbors to see them in a squad car escorted by a sheriff, even if it was for only a block.

"So, do you lock up the pool area every night?"

She shook her head. "No, we have a security guard from eleven to seven and he takes care of that."

Jim nodded. That was good. A female shouldn't be out alone at night, even in this exclusive neighborhood.

The street was lined with flowering trees and the sidewalks were bricked instead of concrete. Pleasant. He was enjoying the walk - and the nicely shaped bikini beside him didn't hurt.

"What time does he lock up?"

"I'm not sure." She wrinkled her nose as well as her forehead. "Maybe at midnight?" She shook her head. "You'll have to ask him. I have his number too."

Angie turned into a walkway leading to a brick home. Every house in the subdivision was large and this one was no exception.

She led him along the path which curved to the right of the house and extended through a gate. She explained. "I never go in the front door." She pulled out her key and they entered a family room that looked out on the back yard when the draperies were open. She pulled them back now and light flooded the room. "I live alone so I keep the drapes closed at night."

Jim didn't want to question her about her marital status, so he said nothing.

He didn't need to. "My husband died three years ago. I open the pool and do all the clerical work in ex-change for my association fees. It helps. There's a lot of upkeep and expenses on this house but I make it - just barely."

He followed her down a hallway to a room that con-tained a computer and desk. From the top drawer of a file cabinet in the corner, she pulled out a manila fold-er and gave him Susan Anderson's cell phone number.

When there was no answer, he didn't leave a mes-sage.

"What kind of a car was she driving?"

"Her BMW – it's white."

Jim called the office. A few minutes later they phoned back with the information he'd asked for. He instructed, "Don't stop the car or approach her when you find it, just let me know the location."

When he hit disconnect, he turned back to Angie Lee. "Paul Adams – is Paul his first name?"

Tears filled her eyes again and she shook her head. "No, it's Stephen. I think it's Stephen." She opened the file folder again. "S. Paul Adams is the way he's listed in the association directory. But I'm pretty sure the S stands for Stephen."

He nodded. That explained what the deputy reported. After Jim wrote down the caretaker's name, address, and number, he could think of no more reasons to stay there with the attractive widow.

Jim Murray loved his job as Sheriff of Franklin County and living in the town of Frankfort where he had grown up. While they were still alive, his parents let him know how disappointed they were. He reminded them that he was still working in the area of the law, but that did not impress his attorney father or his socialite mother. And Carrie, his wife, had turned out to be a real bust. Not the woman for him.

Women. They were always his downfall. So far, his choice of female companions had left a bad taste in his mouth. Carrie turned out to be a snob, interested in the law student but completely disgusted by the law officer. Belinda, who he had dated some in high school, couldn't or wouldn't wait for him to return from college, and married the first person who asked her. She now had four children according to the high school newsletter.

But one of these days Jim knew he'd find the perfect woman. He thought he had once, but that was when he was just a kid. Best not to think about that.

And hey, maybe today was the day. The bikini still hovered in his mind. *Lord, what is wrong with me? I'm tired of thinking about women's bodies!*

He pulled into his designated parking place behind the courthouse. He admitted to himself that his adrenalin was flowing. There was so much about his job that was mundane. But a crime of passion to solve was exciting. *Sorry Lord. A man has been murdered. I shouldn't be enjoying it.*

He'd get Hank Mills, his second deputy, to accompany him while he talked to the caretaker for Windy Hills Estates. When he entered the office, Hank turned from the file cabinet and grinned. "Hey, boss. Did the name jive?"

Jim nodded. "Yeah, the guy went by his middle name. Go with me to talk to the night watchman?"

A few minutes later, they pulled up to the address Angie Lee gave him. But instead of immediately walking to the porch, Jim punched the number into his cell phone.

He figured the guy would be asleep after working all night and wanted to give the courtesy phone call before showing up at the door. Sure enough, the voice that answered sounded sleepy.

"Mr. Coates? Will Coates?" When the voice agreed that he was the desired party, Jim continued. "I'm the Sheriff here and need to ask you some questions about Windy Hills. May my deputy and I come in? We're parked in your driveway."

After the few minutes he requested in order to get dressed, Will Coates appeared in the doorway and Jim and Hank left the squad car.

Coates looked at them with obvious curiosity but pointed to chairs in the small living room without asking any questions.

Jim didn't waste any time with niceties. "Stephen Paul Adams was found in the Windy Hills pool this morning with his throat slit."

The way Coates' eyes bugged, he was either prepared to look shocked, or he really was.

Watching him closely, Jim continued. "We need to know when you locked up the pool area last night and if you noticed anything unusual at that time or later."

Will Coates was shaking his head. "Whew! Throat slit? That...that's bad." He swallowed and took a deep breath. "I usually lock up at midnight but last night it was about twenty after. I remember because I broke up a cat fight and returned Clarence to Mr. and Mrs. Williamson. She wanted to talk about her cat. She always does." He exhibited a slight smile. "When I left there I looked at my watch and saw I was twenty minutes late to secure the gate." Then he shrugged his shoulders. "Not that it matters when I do it. I always check to see if anybody's taking a late-night swim. Doesn't happen often but if so, I come back later."

"Do you ever check the area after you lock up?"

The man shook his head. "Never. No need." Then his eyes widened. "Well, I guess maybe there was a need last night, huh?"

"What do you do after locking the pool gate?"

The grin was sheepish. "I usually go over to the clubhouse. They've got a giant flat screen TV and lots of movies on DVD. I patrol from eleven to midnight and then watch a movie for an hour or so and drive around the neighborhood again for about twenty minutes, go back and finish the movie. Take turns all night. Guarding the clubhouse is one of the most important parts of my job. They've got a well-stocked liquor cabinet and lots of equipment." He paused. "I might as well tell you. I screwed up last night."

"Oh?"

"I'm supposed to vacuum the pool every morning at 6, before I go off duty. And on Monday mornings I backwash the filters."

"But?"

"I did the filters yesterday but didn't vacuum this morning. I fell asleep. Think I'm coming down with something. Just came on home."

"But everyone would have expected you to vacuum the pool at six?"

He nodded as he grimaced. "Guess they'll know now I didn't."

"Who besides you and Ms. Lee have a key to the pool area and clubhouse?"

"All the residents have access to the clubhouse. But not the pool. They were afraid kids would get their parents' keys and somebody might get hurt. They keep the liquor at the clubhouse under a separate lock, so I guess they didn't worry about 'em getting into that."

Jim asked the question that puzzled him from the moment he entered Windy Hills. "Why isn't this a gated community?"

Will Coates threw up both hands. "You'd think, wouldn't you?"

Jim returned to his original question. "Who has keys to the pool?"

"I don't know. Mrs. Lee should be able to tell you."

"And you saw nothing strange at all when you locked up? You looked at the pool to see if anybody was swimming?"

"Yes, sir. I always do. Nobody was there."

"And the lounge chairs? Were they all in order?"

The night watchman looked at him strangely but quickly answered. "I don't know what you mean by in order, but nothing was different than usual."

When they left Will Coates, Jim dropped Hank off at the office and headed back to Windy Hills. He should've asked Angie Lee about the keys while he was there earlier but was glad he had an excuse to go back.

Angie looked awful when she opened the door. Obviously been crying. A lot. She'd changed into sweats and the term "hidden assets" came to his mind. Standing in the doorway, looking all wrung out and pale except for the red rims around her eyes, she stared at him without saying anything.

"I need to ask you another question or two. May I come in?"

She moved aside, but there was nothing welcoming in her body language.

"Ma'am, I need to know everyone who has keys to the pool area."

Color sprang to the pale face. "Just me and the night guard and the president of the association."

"Who is the president?"

"Sydney White. He is the original owner of the land and he developed the subdivision."

"His address?" When he had the information, he needed to locate Sydney White, he asked another question.

"How do you think Mr. Adams gained entry to the area after it was locked?"

She shook her head. "I don't know." Tears welled up in her eyes again.

His cell phone began singing "Home on the Range" to inform him that the office was calling. When he hung up he turned back to Angie Lee. "They've located Mrs. Adams having lunch. Would you want to go with me to tell her?"

The woman's eyes widened with a look of horror. "No! Please. I...I can't. I don't have to, do I?"

"No. Of course not. I just thought maybe someone she knows – it would be easier." He turned back. "And I meant to ask you earlier. Was that lounge chair half way in the pool when you got there, or did it happen later?"

"It was there. That was the first thing that made me think something was wrong. And then when I looked in..." The tears welled up again.

As soon as he got in the car, he called the city police and asked for the assistance of Officer Helen Bailey. She was on duty and could meet him. Letting the female officer accompany the Sheriff on missions involving other females was a courtesy from the city that he really appreciated. He'd decided to get a female deputy when money came available to add another position.

As he pulled into the Staxx BBQ parking lot, he spotted the white BMW right away. And there was an empty space beside it. Glancing into the car, he saw books scattered on the back seat and floor. It wasn't long before Helen joined him. They were parked next to the empty building between Staxx and Captain D's on Hudson Hollow.

"I hate to go in and tell her during lunch – in front of everybody. Wanna grab a bite while we wait for her to finish?" His stomach was growling, and he realized it had been over six hours since breakfast.

Helen grinned. She was a perky brunette, kind of pretty and a lot of fun but not his type. He preferred blondes for one thing.

"I'd just as soon wait 'til we've told her and taken her home. Then we wouldn't have to hurry and maybe have to leave half of it sitting there."

"Yeah, that'd be nice but I'm hungry now. Why don't I walk over to Captain D's and get something and bring it back? We can sit in my car and eat."

She shrugged. "Okay. I want clams with corn on the cob and steamed broccoli."

"Steamed broccoli?" Fries and Cole Slaw for him.

"Steamed broccoli." She said it firmly.

They'd just finished eating and were stuffing garbage in the bag when Mrs. Adams walked out of the restaurant carrying a purse in one hand and a book in the other. Her hair was gray and pulled into a bun at the back of her neck. When she unlocked the car beside Jim's, they knew for sure it was her. With a 'here goes' glance at each other, they got out of the car.

"Mrs. Adams?" Jim purposefully made his tone gentle.

The woman looked startled, and her eyes widened further when she spotted Helen who was in uniform. She nodded and clutched the book close to her chest.

"I'm Sheriff Jim Murray. We've been waiting for you because we have some bad news."

"Bad news?"

"Yes, Ma'am. It's about your husband."

"He's had a heart attack?"

"No, Ma'am. But he is…deceased. His body was found in the Windy Acres pool."

She frowned. "I don't understand. I thought he was at work."

Didn't she hear what he was telling her? "No, Ma'am. When was the last time you saw him?"

"Last night. I always go to bed at eleven. We said good night then."

"You have separate bedrooms?"

She squared her shoulders and her eyes narrowed, but she answered his question. "Yes. We require different types of mattresses."

"Mrs. Adams, we're very sorry for your loss and Officer Bailey will be happy to drive you home. You'll want to call your daughter and we can talk further there."

Susan Adams frowned. "But I have a whole list of things I need to do today."

Shock. Hasn't taken it in yet. He made his voice even more gentle – but firm. "Yes, Ma'am, but they can wait."

Chapter Two

"Horses sweat, men perspire, and ladies merely glow." Polly remembered her mother's quote as she watched shoppers avidly examine the overflowing tables in RiversEdge Campground's shelter house.

There was much glowing and some perspiring happening.

She'd hoped for a lot of customers for her garage/yard/whatever sale, but this exceeded her greatest expectations. A breeze would have been nice, but it was almost worth the stifling heat to see the excitement over the contents of her former home and lately, storage unit.

Her new friend Brenda was busily taking money and giving change. Brenda grinned and gave her a thumbs up before turning to the next customer.

"How much is this set of dishes?" A whiney voice interrupted Polly's moment of triumph. Rejecting the urge to respond with impatience, she smiled and pointed to the sign beside the Blue Willow that clearly declared the set to be $80.00.

She thought of the bumper sticker Walter threatened to put on his car - "Stupid people shouldn't be allowed air." Of course he was joking. Walter would never have done anything to mar his image as the brilliant and sophisticated attorney that he worked so hard to attain.

By 2:30 p.m. the place cleared out and Polly breathed a sigh of relief. They had been there since 9 a.m. Maybe they could close up? So, what if she still had a bunch of stuff? She could donate it somewhere.

"Thank you so much, Brenda. I really appreciate your help."

"It's fun. But doesn't it bother you to get rid of all your nice things? We've always lived in a trailer, until we got the motor home, and I can't imagine giving up a real house and all ... " She waved her hand at the ghosts of the things that covered the tables that morning.

Polly shook her head. "Not really. I was ready for it. I'm so glad to be free – free from my ex and free from my job. When I turned sixty-two in January, I couldn't wait to retire and thought I'd love staying home, but frankly, I'm glad to be free from my house too. The upkeep and yard work – too much to handle alone. I'm relieved to downsize." She'd done it again – my ex. Walter refused to walk out of her thoughts and conversation just yet. She'd be glad when he did. He had no problem walking out of her life and into the arms of his new young wife.

"I'm glad you decided to buy into the Campground. We needed you around here." Brenda's statement came as a complete shock to Polly who saw herself as the needy one, grateful that the other stockholders of RiversEdge included her and, in the six weeks trial period since she moved here the middle of April, made her feel like one of them. She'd only been here seven weeks and it already felt like home.

"How could you need me? I don't add anything."

Brenda smiled and patted her shoulder. "Believe me, you do."

The screen door opened, and a very thin, pale-skinned woman entered. She had on a different floppy hat than the one worn several days ago when they played Spades together with a group in the shelter house. The woman seemed nice, and in a soft southern accent told them she came to the Frankfort area to see some kind of exhibit and was staying until the weekend. Polly wished she could remember her name.

"Hi." The thin woman granted her wish. "I'm Gretchen Anderson. We met the other day."

Polly smiled and nodded gratefully. "And I'm Polly Nichols."

"I thought I was stayin' 'til Saturday but found out last night I need to go help a friend. I thought I'd stop by and check out your stuff on my way out."

Brenda stepped up and held out her hand. "I'm Brenda Croft. Sorry to meet you just as you're leaving. Maybe you can come back sometime."

Gretchen shrugged as their hands unclasped. "You never know. There's a lot to explore in this area. I may get back here someday. I'm from Georgia." Her eyes wandered over the tables and she moved to the kitchen section.

Polly saw her pick up a skillet. A strange man nodded to Polly and Brenda as he came in the door. He walked over to Gretchen.

Polly saw the two talking and watched as Gretchen laid down the black iron skillet and pick up the other small one. She nodded approval. If she hadn't had two of them, that skillet would never have ended up in the sale. It was a real bargain ... Pampered Chef. She'd bought two because she and Walter liked different kinds of omelets. He liked sausage, green peppers, onions, tomatoes, and hot sauce in his and she wanted mushroom and cheese only. So now Walter's omelet pan was going out of her life just as surely as he did.

Polly turned back to Brenda at the table where she sat counting money. "Have we taken in much?"

"Just a minute." Brenda finished stacking the bills. "According to what I've counted, subtracting the hundred you started with, you've already made over five hundred dollars."

"Wow! That's amazing." Polly grinned. "I confess I've never had a yard sale before, so I didn't know what to expect."

Gretchen came up to the table, the skillet in one hand and a map book in the other.

Polly smiled at her. "We sure hate to see you go. Are you sure you can't stick around another week?"

"I had hoped to, but my friend is having surgery and she needs my help. Can I set my stuff on the table while I keep looking?"

Polly laughed. "You go right ahead. Buy as much as you like!'

"Have you sold a lot?"

"Much better than we expected."

Gretchen moved back toward the tables and in a short time came back with two Wordsmith games un-

17

der her arm.

Polly didn't hide her surprise. "Are you sure you want both of these? I honestly don't know where the new one came from. I can't remember having it. The old box was mine, but it's not in very good shape."

"Yes, I'll keep that one for myself, and I plan to give the other one to my friend Peg. We're both wordsmiths, well we try to be." She grinned.

Polly nodded, "Then you should love this game." She smiled at Gretchen who promptly handed Brenda $15 for the purchases.

"Have a great trip. I hope you enjoy the games – and the skillet."

"Thanks. I hope you make lots of money in your sale."

Before the door closed behind the departing camper, a new influx of shoppers appeared, and it was nearly five before the place cleared out again.

"Well?" Brenda stretched and put a hand to her back. "Think that's all?"

"I hope so. I'm hungry."

"We could take some of your profit and go into town and splurge on Chinese. I don't have to cook tonight cause Doug's working late."

"That is a great idea. You've sure earned it." Polly looked around at the tables, which had very few items left on them. "But I guess we better clean this up first. There will be people coming to play cards before we get back." She'd only been given one day for her sale and it couldn't be on a weekend because every night and all day on weekends the shelter house was filled with people playing cards or games of some kind.

Brenda nodded and began gathering the leftover

goods into a wicker laundry basket while Polly folded tables.

"Oh, and take anything you want, Brenda."

"Are you sure you don't want the Getting Home game? It's still in the wrapper, the old version made decades ago. It could be worth a lot."

"I don't want it. I kept out the one game I love - Victim. I played it a lot with my Daddy when I was a kid. Just couldn't bring myself to get rid of it. What will you do with the Getting Home?"

"Sell it on e-bay. I sell lots of stuff but kinda specialize in games. My user id is even FunGameMama."

Polly laughed. "Are you serious? FunGameMama?"

"Yep. That's me."

Polly and Brenda sat a little apart from the others out on the grass beyond the concrete floor of the lower pavilion and watched their neighbors perform with greater and lesser degrees of talent. Tuesday nights were for Karaoke. Dot Broughton pulled a chair over close to them.

"Mind if I join you? Tom's covering the office." Dot was the manager's ex-wife. She still worked behind the desk as she had when they were married, but since the breakup six months ago, they lived in separate campers. The divorced couple didn't seem at all awkward about continuing to work together, and the rest of the residents were adapting to the situation.

"Of course not." In a gesture of welcome, Polly scooted her chair over to make room.

Just as Dot sat down, a new performer stepped up

to the platform. Jill Trent wore a low-cut top that left no doubt about the authenticity of her bra size. The three older women exchanged looks but no one commented.

To Polly's surprise the woman had a wonderfully rich voice. She chose a blues number from the forties, and her execution sounded much like the original artist. Polly had a flashback of sitting around a piano bar trying to enjoy a singer and ignore Walter as he flirted with the redhead seated on the other side of him.

Dot stood up abruptly. "I think I'll go up to the shelter house and see what's going on there."

"I'll join you." Polly rose and folded up her own aluminum lawn chair.

"Me too." Brenda followed.

Polly cleared her throat as they walked to the upper campground. "I don't suppose I could talk you guys into playing my Victim game with me, could I?"

"Suits me." That from Dot.

"Me too," Brenda added.

Polly giggled. "I couldn't make myself sell it and I've been itching to play. It was my favorite game when I was a kid."

The shelter house was already inhabited by the inevitable Bridge Bunch. The foursome, Lucy and George Riley, Col. Clayton Wylie, and Sam Molloy were engrossed in their nightly game. Lucy looked up briefly when the screen door opened. She acknowledged their presence with a gracious nod and slight smile before returning her attention to the cards in her hand. The Bridge Bunch were all older than the majority of campers who ranged from their forties to mid-sixties. They were probably in their late seventies. And all very dignified, with the exception of Sam Molloy. Where the Colonel was most definitely spit-shine and military, and the Riley's definitely country-club and name brand, Sam was laid back. His hair was usually hanging over his ears in little wispy white strands and his clothes old, comfortable, and sometimes needed mending.

"I'll go get the game." Polly took her lawn chair and left the other two women setting up a second card table and folding chairs while she hurried through the dark to her camper. The music that drifted up from the pavilion proclaimed that Jill Trent was still performing and doing it very well. The applause at the end of her second number encouraged her to start a third. Polly paused at the door to her camper and looked back toward the shelter. It was bathed in the golden glow of the streetlights. She loved this place.

When Polly came out of the camper again she took a few minutes of basking in the cricket sounds that accompanied the music before she returned to the shelter, Victim game in one hand and a tin box in the other.

"I brought some homemade brownies." She set the tin on the table.

Brenda laughed and held up a plate and stack of napkins. "I ran to our camper and got chocolate chip cookies."

Dot lifted her eyebrows. "If I hang around you two very long, I'll never get in shape to snag another husband."

"Do you really want one?" Polly felt the blood rush to her face, but the other woman laughed. "I'm sorry. I can't imagine wanting to be married again." She looked apologetically at Brenda, the only married one of the bunch.

"I understand. Don't mind me. There are moments. But with all his faults, I can't imagine life without Doug. We've been together since high school."

Dot shook her head. "I was Tom's third wife. I should have known."

Polly didn't say anything; during her first week there, Brenda filled her in on the campground manager's obsession with women that led to the divorce. She picked up some napkins and the brownies.

"How about a snack?" She held out her offerings to the Bridge players as she crossed the space between the two tables.

The single men reached for the dessert like they'd been eagerly waiting for the chance. Lucy and George declined with their usual dignity.

After the three women settled themselves with chocolate treats and bottled water from the machine, they unpacked the Victim box.

"Let the games begin!" Polly cheerfully announced.

Soon they were completely engrossed in the familiar old game. Polly chose to be the Cook, Brenda the Musician, and Dot the Artist. Dot seemed to land on more than her share of safety zones while Brenda got more than her share of hazards. Polly felt the familiar childhood thrill when she landed on the amusement park. It was nearly midnight when the three packed up the game and agreed to meet the next morning and play again.

On the way back to her camper, Polly realized the lower pavilion was now dark and silent. A shudder ran through her body.

Chapter Three

While Helen was driving the widow back to Windy Acres, Jim called the coroner. "Hey, it's me. Can they tell if the Adams guy had sex shortly before his death?"

"It depends. They can measure semen and see if the normal amount is depleted but that wouldn't be foolproof because it can vary sometimes, depending on testosterone level."

"Crap. But they will do the measuring?"

"If it's requested. Want me to call down there?"

"Yeah. And how close do you think they can get to time of death?"

"Because of the body being in water, not too close. Probably within a few hours."

Jim sighed. "Thanks. Let me know." He didn't like the thought that came to his mind when he met the widow Adams. Comparing her to the widow Lee, who had a key to the pool, he knew which he'd rather be with in the middle of the night. But he shook his head. He had to stop thinking like that. He'd just found a new church and was trying to change his life and submit everything to God. Sometimes he just couldn't make it work.

They got Susan Adams home and sat with her while she phoned her daughter. At one point, she handed her cell phone to him. He was surprised when she left the room but glad that he could speak freely. "I'm sorry about your father."

"What happened?"

"I haven't told the details to your mother. She seems to be in a state of shock, not taking it in."

"That's Mom. She doesn't take in much. Lives in her own little world." Jim could hear the bitterness in her voice, even in the midst of what had to be sorrow for the loss of her father.

"It was not an accident." He felt a need to break the news gently.

"Tell me." The voice sounded ready to hear anything.

"He was found across the street in the pool, with his throat cut."

The gasp that came through the phone showed him that Paul Adams' daughter had not expected that.

"I'm sorry," he repeated.

"I'll be there on the first flight I can get."

"Do you want to talk to your mother again?"

"No, I'll phone her when I know my arrival time."

They offered to do anything they could to help Mrs. Adams and she asked them to carry in the books from her car that was now parked in the garage. As he stacked them, he saw that they were all romance novels. The women on the front looked more like Angie Lee than Susan Adams.

Jim drove Helen back to her car in the Staxx parking lot and thanked her for her help.

"Strange lady," was her response.

"Not just in shock, you think?"

"Uh uh. It's more than that."

"Her daughter said she quote 'doesn't take in much' unquote."

Helen nodded and then waved as she got in her patrol car.

Jim watched until she drove away and then hit himself in the forehead with his fist. He'd left Tony Morales locked in the Windy Hills pool area without lunch.

He drove through and got another order from Captain D's. And hoped Tony liked fish.

When Angie Lee appeared at her front door in answer to his ring she looked a little better, although she still had on the sweats. Jim explained about needing the key. "I'll get one made so I won't have to keep bothering you."

"Just keep it. I'm not going to be unlocking for a long time. They can either get Will to do it or have more keys made."

Crime Scene tape had to be moved slightly to unlock the gate. Morales was glad to see him and even more glad to see the late lunch. When he'd finished eating, they walked around the area and tried to reconstruct the murder scene.

Morales pointed to the overturned lounge chair at the edge of the pool. "You can see a trace of blood there." He pointed to the arm rest. "Not much. But if he was dumped right after being cut, just a slight bit might get spilled there."

Jim nodded. "No sign of the murder weapon?"

The deputy shook his head. "And I've been through everything – trash containers, flower bed, everything."

They were interrupted by the arrival of Deputy Mills. Jim unlocked the gate and let him in – and put the tape back before relocking the gate.

When the three had examined everything, they saw to inspect in the area, they left. The two deputies parted to go from house to house to ask questions as well as give residents the news of their neighbor's death and the closure of the pool.

Jim headed downtown to the bank. The president of Windy Hills was also the president of First Security Investment Bank and Trust Company.

When he showed his badge, the secretary's haughty expression changed slightly. "I'll check." She left her desk and after a brief knock, entered through the inner door to his right. Jim looked around the plush office. Nice – and this was just the reception area. There was a horse theme, lots of pictures of Keeneland Race Track, leather replicas of horses on a table by the window.

"Mr. White will see you." The attractive blonde stood aside as he walked into the inner office. She closed the door behind him.

Sydney White stood up from behind a desk covered with papers. He didn't come out but reached across to shake hands.

Jim seated himself in the chair Mr. White indicated. "I'm sorry to bother you, Sir, but there's been some trouble at Windy Hills."

Alarm sprang to the banker's face. "Vandals?"

"No sir. Worse. A murder."

White's face turned pale. "Who?"

"Paul Adams."

Was it relief he saw in the banker's eyes?

Sydney White shook his head. "But how?"

"He was found in the pool with his throat slit."

"In the pool?" The man half rose from his chair and sat back down. "When?"

"Ms. Lee found him when she unlocked the gate this morning. I'm surprised she hasn't called you."

"Me too." White's face flushed. "I mean, she should have reported it."

"She was pretty shook up. Oh, and I have her key. She said she wouldn't be unlocking for a while."

The banker nodded. Then he looked at Jim expectantly.

"I'm trying to track down keys. There's Ms. Lee and Will Coates and you. Anybody else?"

White shook his head. "Not that I know of. We decided to stick to regular hours and not have a lot of keys floating around, for security reasons." He gave a short laugh. "Doesn't seem to have done much good, does it?"

"Do you have any idea how Mr. Adams would have gained access to the area?"

Sydney White looked up at the ceiling for a few seconds. "No. Can't think of a thing."

"Where is your key, Mr. White?"

He pulled a set out of his pocket. When he'd sorted through the ring, he set one apart. "This one."

"When's the last time you used it?"

"Never."

"You've never used the key at all?"

He shook his head. "No need. I don't swim. And my wife doesn't either. The pool was a later addition. In the beginning I just built the clubhouse. But our daughter begged for a pool and so did the rest of the association."

"Sir, do you know why anyone would want to kill Mr. Adams?"

The innocence in the banker's wide blue eyes was remarkable. "I have no idea. Paul Adams was well thought of in the community. Solid citizen. Owns Adams' Insurance."

"What about other women? Was he faithful to his wife?"

The gaze fell to the desk. "I wouldn't know about that." Jim would make a bet that he would know about that.

"And I'd like to ask another question, if I may. Just out of curiosity. I understand you developed Windy Hills?"

White lifted his eyes and leaned back in his chair. "Yes, about fifteen years ago. It was a lifelong dream of mine."

"Why didn't you make it a gated community?"

The gaze wandered over to the wall full of pictures of the banker posing with various state government officials. "Just seemed like a lot of trouble. I'd rather go in and out of my own home without bothering to stop and check in with anybody. The night security takes care of any safety issues from outsiders since the clubhouse is right by the entrance and he head-quarters there during the night when he's not patrol-ling."

"So, if it's safe from outsiders, you are assuming that whoever killed Mr. Adams is a resident of Windy Hills?"

The blue eyes narrowed. "No." He was quiet for several seconds. "Hey, why didn't Coates find the body?"

"He was sick and went on home without vacuum-ing the pool at six."

"Hm. Wonder how often he does that?"

Jim decided he wouldn't want to be derelict in the cold eyes of Sydney White. He stood up and put his notebook back in his pocket.

"Thank you for your time, Mr. White. We'll be out of your pool area by tomorrow evening at the latest. And..." He searched for inoffensive words. "I'm sure you'll want to drain and clean the pool before re-opening for the residents."

A puzzled look appeared and then dissolved into understanding. The banker nodded.

"And please contact me if you think of anything that would help us find a motive for Mr. Adam's mur-der."

Jim turned back as he went through the door and saw Sydney White picking up the telephone.

The microwave signaled that his hot dogs were ready just as the cell phone rang. It was the coroner.

"We got lucky. Not many murders today."

"And?" Jim's stomach muscles tightened.

"Either the guy had a very low testosterone count, or he'd had sex shortly before death."

"Time?"

"Window of one to three a.m. Death from loss of blood due to severed carotid artery."

"Weapon?"

"Interesting. Said it looked like a serrated blade."

Jim's brain raced as he clipped the cell phone back in his belt holder. Serrated blade. Kitchen knife? He couldn't get warrants to search every kitchen in Windy Hills. And it would probably be gone by now anyway.

He got the phone back out and pulled up the Adams phone number that he'd programmed in earlier. When Susan Adams answered he identified himself and asked about her daughter.

"She'll be here around ten tonight. She flies into Lexington and will rent a car."

"Are you all right, Ma'am?"

"Yes. I'm fine." And after several seconds of silence, "Thank you."

"When would be a good time for me to come by tomorrow to talk to the two of you?"

"I don't know. Stephanie will be tired of course. But she'll probably have questions. Maybe ten o'clock?"

"Or ten thirty."

"Ten o'clock would be better. A nice complete number, don't you think?"

Weird. But – some girls, they said, were a perfect ten. Most fell something short of that. "Ten it is." He put the phone back in the holder, this time shaking his head. He'd like to look through her kitchen. As

Helen Bailey said, strange lady. But that wasn't a good enough reason to get the judge to issue a search warrant. Sticky situation about the sex thing. He'd need to get Helen back to question the wife. Maybe while he was talking to the daughter tomorrow morning.

Susan Adams stared helplessly around the kitchen. She ought to be planning something for her daughter to eat. There'd be three meals tomorrow and every day after that. For how long? She hadn't thought to ask. Her heart pounded unpleasantly. She hoped it wouldn't be too long. And the funeral. Do people come to the house after a funeral and expect to be fed? At least Stephanie could handle all that. The sheriff asked if she wanted to call her preacher or something. She didn't tell him she didn't have a preacher, that Paul didn't believe in church.

The phone rang again. The voice on the other end introduced himself as the coroner and asked which mortuary she wanted her husband's body taken to. The last funeral she'd attended was at Rogers so she gave him that name.

She turned her attention to the matter of food again and opened the pantry to search through the shelves. What if Stephanie came in hungry tonight? There were some cans of soup. Mushroom, tomato, French onion. But didn't Stephanie like chicken noodle best? Maybe she'd better run out to the store. Susan sighed just as the phone rang for the third time in a half hour.

It was Rogers Funeral Home. No, she couldn't be there at 10 but she and her daughter should be able to come in at 12.

Susan looked sadly at the coffee pot. There could be no coffee and card left for her from Stevie tomorrow morning.

Officer Bailey was free and would meet him at the Adams house at ten a.m. That was a relief. Jim drove through McDonalds and ordered a sausage and egg biscuit to take to the office with him. After winning a micro-struggle with his better judgment, he added a second sandwich and some hash browns. That was one good thing about being single. He didn't have some woman fussing about his fat and carbohydrate intake like Hank and Tony. But then he didn't have the benefits they did either.

Both deputies were in the courthouse that morning and both made noises about his unhealthy breakfast. He knew it was just jealousy. Morales sure tucked into the fried fish and potatoes yesterday. And he saw Hank eat two Big Macs when the derailment kept them out over suppertime a few weeks ago.

Jim just grinned. "Sure is good though." He enjoyed every bite chewed in front of the deputies. Hank admitted to having oatmeal and bananas that morning and Tony had eaten cornflakes.

When he asked the deputy to compile a list of Windy Hills residents, Hank handed him a sheet of paper. He should have known it would already be done; these guys made his job easy. Tony was perfect at scene-of-crime and nobody could beat Hank at research. He often reminded himself that one of the signs of a good boss was knowing who to hire and how to delegate. It helped drive away feelings of inferiority.

Jim parked at the curb outside the Adams house and waited until Helen Bailey pulled up behind him. She really was a good-looking woman but too self-assured for him to be interested in a relationship. He liked his women more vulnerable.

The door was opened by a gorgeous blonde and for a minute Jim was speechless. From seeing the mother, he'd not expected this.

"Sheriff Murray?"

He nodded. And swallowed. "Stephanie Adams?"

When she inclined her head in agreement, he introduced the police officer and they were ushered into the living room.

Susan Adams sat on the couch, her face a study in non-expression. Her daughter waved them toward two chairs facing the sofa, before joining her mother.

Jim noted that they sat on opposite ends of the couch. He'd expected the daughter to sit next to her mother and hold her hand or something. Maybe they'd already done all that crying and comforting stuff.

Stephanie opened the conversation. "I hope you won't take too long, Sheriff. We have to go to the funeral home and there are a lot of phone calls to make."

He nodded. "I understand. And hope we can get all the information we need quickly." He looked over at Helen.

The officer smiled across the room. "Mrs. Adams, could you and I talk privately in your kitchen for a few minutes?"

Susan Adams did not appear to mind at all.

When he was alone with Stephanie, he leaned back

against the cushiony chair. "How is your mother doing?"

She shrugged. "Like always. Very well." She sighed. "You see, my mother lives in her own little world. Nothing much affects her."

He frowned. "Not even her husband's death?"

Stephanie appeared to think for several seconds. "Not even that. She doesn't get emotional about anything. Her biggest concern right now seems to be how to feed me for the time I'm in."

Different. Definitely different.

"Miss Adams..." He paused. "Is it Miss Adams or are you married?"

Her lips curled up at the corners. "Miss Adams it is."

"Do you know of any reason why your father would be murdered? Did he have enemies?"

She shook her head vigorously. "No. Not at all. My father was a wonderful man. Honest, fair. A good man." She said it with finality and a look that dared him to question her pronouncement.

He didn't.

"Did your parents have a happy marriage?"

She emitted a snort of laughter. "No. But it wasn't a bad marriage. No fighting or anything like that. Just boring."

"So, do you think your father would have had relationships with other women?"

She tilted her head to one side. "You don't really think I'd know about that, do you, Sheriff?" Her eyes twinkled.

He answered her grin with his own. "Guess not. But it was worth a try."

"As it turns out, you win."

He frowned. "What do you mean?"

"I mean I do know about that. When I was in high school my best friend and I found out that my father and her mother were lovers." She shrugged. "When I confronted him, he acted ashamed but he didn't say he was sorry. I understood."

"You did?" That was unusual for a kid.

"I told you, my mother is emotionless. That would have to get old, even for a male."

Obviously, her opinion of men was not real high. He pulled the notebook out of his pocket.

"Can you give me the name of the woman? The mother of your friend?"

She smiled. "I can. But I'd rather not."

He leaned back in the chair again. "Without the name, we'll have to ask questions of people and that always causes more talk and speculation in the community."

"You win again! The woman was Margaret White."

Whoa! "The banker's wife?"

"Bingo."

"Anything else to tell me?"

"Not a thing, Sheriff."

"How often do you fly in to visit your parents?"

The cocky look disappeared. "Not often." She shook her head. "As it happens, I was coming in next week. Dad asked me. I'm sorry I didn't get to see him."

Ah, a chink in the armor. Loves her Dad. He got up from the chair. "I told Officer Morgan we'd join them in the kitchen when we were through talking."

"And what was she going to try and worm out of my mother? Details of the sex life of The Adams Family?"

This one was a sharp cookie. Jim didn't respond.

When they reached the kitchen, Helen looked up at him and gave a slight nod.

"Thank you, Mrs. Adams, Miss Adams," he said. "We appreciate your cooperation." He pulled out his wallet and extracted a card that he handed to the daughter. "Call me if you think of anything or if I can be of help."

Stephanie took the card and nodded. "Will do."

"Sheriff!" Susan Adam's voice caused him to turn around just as he was going through to the hallway.

"Yes, Ma'am?"

"When will the pool be open again? I went over last night and saw the police tape."

She went over last night? "Umm, Ma'am, I don't know. When we vacate the premises, I'll tell Mr. White. And I'm sure he'll inform the neighborhood when the pool is available."

She nodded. "Thank you."

As they walked away from the house, he said to Helen in a low voice, "We can't stand out here and talk about them in full view. Want to come over to the office?"

"I'd rather go get coffee."

"Where?"

"MacDonald's okay?"

"See you there."

As soon as they were seated in a corner booth, Helen reported. "They haven't had sex for years."

He nodded. "Not surprised. The daughter says he's been cheating since she was in high school."

"Scum." Helen spat out the word. She picked up

the coffee cup with both hands and took a sip. "Men!"

"What do you mean, men? Like we're some kind of disease or something."

She gave him a strange look.

"What?"

"I saw the way you looked at the daughter."

"So? She's a beautiful woman. What's the harm?"

The police officer just shook her head.

Chapter Four

That Friday Polly settled in the folding chair and smiled at her two game partners.

She was glad that the extension phone located in the shelter house made it convenient for Dot to join them. When she was not actually waiting on someone, she could visit and answer the office calls from there.

"Hey!" Dot looked around. "We're the only ones here. Great!"

"That probably won't last long." Brenda sat in the chair where she'd been the night before. "Let's get started. I thought about this game all night. Even dreamed that I was the Musician – a sexy Blues Singer." She laughed. "Wishful thinking. I have no talent."

"That would be Jill Trent, don't you think?"

Polly looked up, slightly startled at the sarcasm in Dot's voice. Brenda seemed not to notice.

"Yeah, guess so." Brenda sighed dramatically. Then she laughed. "Who's most like our game characters? I think you're right and Jill is definitely the Musician.

Who would Bill be?"

"The Salesman." Polly responded almost without thinking. She didn't realize until she said it that she viewed the man as pushy.

Since no one contradicted her, she guessed they must have the same opinion.

Dot made her contribution. "Lucy Riley is definitely the Artist." When the grande dame was not playing Bridge, she had a needlepoint project going, or could be seen with oil paints and easel out on a bank overlooking the river.

"And George is the Banker. Aren't they wonderful?" Brenda's smile beamed her approval of the campground's oldest and most elegant couple.

"And Col. Wylie is the Soldier, of course." The other two agreed with Polly that was a given.

Dot frowned. "But who is the Secretary?"

Polly glanced at Brenda who was studying her cards. Dot herself was such an obvious choice that any other candidates faded in the background of Polly's mind. Clearly a beauty in her younger days, Dot Broughton had let herself go. The word dowdy came to mind. And though she talked about her ex-husband's previous marriages, the rumor was that she'd been married at least that many times herself and married to former employers. But she was meticulous in her role as secretary of the campground board and in running the office. And what was wrong with being a secretary anyway? But evidently Dot saw herself in some other role.

Brenda saved the day. "What about June Gabbard?" The widowed inhabitant of the camper next to the office was agreed upon as secretary.

Polly recounted their decisions. "We've got June as the Secretary, Col. Wylie as the Soldier, Lucy and George Riley as the Artist and Banker, Bill and Jill Trent as Salesman and Musician." She thought for a minute. "Tom would be the Handyman, even though he is the Manager here. But who would be the Cook? Ah, Sam?" Her voice softened as she named the last one. Sam Molloy always seemed vulnerable to her for some reason.

Dot nodded. "He does love to experiment with casseroles, doesn't he?" At the monthly potluck held in the lower pavilion, Sam always surprised them with very different dishes. "Remember the Apple/Bean Bake?"

Brenda turned to Polly, "That was last summer and actually it wasn't too bad. But the Artichoke okra casserole last month was something else entirely."

"Yuck!" Polly made a face. "I didn't even try it."

Brenda's forehead wrinkled. "But who would be the most likely Victim?"

The many hazards in the game allowed for two defeats for each player, but the third defeat produced the Victim and ended the game.

"It's a shame we don't get to choose." Dot's voice again dripped with sarcasm. But before they could respond, loud voices came through the screen.

"You will not treat my dog like that!" The normally cultured voice of Lucy Riley was shrill with fury.

"Then you'll keep your dog on a leash."

"Mister Broughton, we were here long before you came. And ..."

"I've put up with that mutt running all over the place long enough. The rules say no pets unless they are on leashes."

"That rule was made for part time campers, not for residents."

"It doesn't say that. It just says no pets except on leashes."

The three Victim players looked at each other in shock.

Dot scooted her chair back and stood up. "I'd better see what's going on."

Polly and Brenda watched through the screen as the manager's ex-wife joined him and the Rileys in front of their camper. George had his arm around his wife's shoulders while she held the offending canine tightly to her chest.

Polly turned to Brenda. "I feel like an eavesdropper."

Brenda nodded. "Let's work on the puzzle for a while." The two moved to the opposite side of the shelter where a jigsaw puzzle sat half finished. Puzzle corner was always there for anyone who wanted to fill up a few minutes or hours – a campground group project. This picture was of a thatched roof cottage.

Polly looked thoughtfully at the puzzle. "Wouldn't it be awful if we worked on this all these weeks and then there were some pieces missing and we couldn't finish it."

Brenda frowned. "Yes, definitely frustrating."

After a few minutes Dot joined them, shaking her head. "Someday that temper of Tom's is going to get him in trouble."

Polly was glad when Brenda asked the question. "What happened?"

"He kicked the Riley's dog. And Lucy saw him."

"No wonder she was mad." Polly might not be an avid pet lover, but she strongly disapproved of unkindness to animals. "Why did he kick it?"

"Pepper wandered out of their site and over to the office. As much as I could get, he wasn't doing anything wrong, just standing there. But Tom hates him for some reason. He went out and kicked him. Didn't realize that Lucy was looking out of their camper and just about to go retrieve the dog." She shook her head. "I've never seen the Rileys so upset."

That afternoon the three reluctantly put up the Victim game and prepared to go to their various homes to prepare the evening meal. They promised to resume after dinner.

"But we'll probably be kidded a lot," warned Dot. "The card players will think this game is for kids."

"Their loss!" Polly tossed her head and tucked the beloved box under her arm.

Dot's prophecy proved to be accurate.

"I cannot believe you three! You're actually playing that kid's game?"

Brenda looked up at Jill Trent. "Don't be shy, Jill. Tell us what you really think." Jill wrinkled her nose in a sneer and pulled another card table out from against the wall. When she had it set up with chairs unfolded, she retrieved the pinochle cards from the game box.

There was a Spades game going strong and a Hearts table. There was also a foursome who came every weekend and played Hands and Feet, a Canasta derivative. And of course, the Bridge Bunch.

Whenever Colonel Wylie was dummy, he walked over to add a few pieces to the growing puzzle. Polly felt sorry for him, for some reason she couldn't quite narrow down. Perhaps it was the constant talk about his military career that bordered on bragging. No, it was full bragging, all the way inside the border. She always pitied people who had to try and convince others of their own importance. Maybe that's why she'd stayed with Walter so long. She shook off the thought of Walter once again and returned her concentration to the game.

With six tables of people carrying on conversations there was a medium sized roar that filled the shelter house but after a few minutes, a clear word surfaced above the confusion.

"Sir!" Col. Wylie's voice raised in shock ushered in a startled silence.

When Polly looked around she saw Tom Broughton standing over the Bridge Bunch with a smirk on his face.

"Well, it was a stupid move. Even a non-expert like me could see that."

Lucy Riley closed up the cards in her hand and smiled through tight narrowed lips at her bridge partner. "Clayton, why don't we finish this game in our camper?" Her eyes moved to Sam Molloy and included him in the invitation. George rose from his own chair and pulled out his wife's, assisting her to her feet.

Throughout the room the old timers exchanged glances. Brenda leaned over to Polly and whispered. "The Rileys never invite people to their home. Ever."

When the foursome was gone, Tom walked over to the radio and punched a button. Country music blared out into the room. Polly didn't mind country music, not too much anyway, but she didn't want it while she was concentrating on a game. And she doubted the others did either.

Dot excused herself and went over to where her ex-husband stood beside the machine. No one could hear what she said to him, but he glared and then turned off the music.

"Anybody wants to have a lively Friday night, meet me at the pavilion." He directed his stare right into Jill's eyes. Polly was certain that she wasn't the only one who saw the flush spread over Bill Trent's face.

The Pinochle players must have been on the last hand of their game, for in a few minutes all four left, presumably to meet Tom Broughton at the pavilion. Those who were playing Spades shortly followed suit.

"I expect there'll be a board meeting Monday and an owner's meeting to follow." Dot spoke in a low voice even though there was nobody around to hear her.

"About?"

"About getting rid of Tom. The Rileys have never liked him and they've brought it up before. Back when I was married to him, I'd hear him rant and rave about them. But he's been so efficient on the grounds that the rest of the board talked them into giving him more time. But today..." She shook her head. "I don't know what's wrong with him. He always acted like that in the privacy of our camper but now he's showing his true colors in public. Not like him at all."

Just then, Bill Trent came through the door. "Mind if I join you?"

Polly was shocked. She'd assumed he would stay at the Pavilion to keep an eye on his wife. And it never occurred to her that Bill would want to play what the rest of the campground deemed a childish game.

"Sure, we're just starting a new game. Choose a role." She waved her hand at the pile of 'people' laying there in the box. She carefully did not look at the other two women when Bill picked up the little man carrying a briefcase stamped 'sales'.

"I remember playing this as a boy. I liked the feeling of being The Survivor."

The others nodded agreement. The main object of the game was to avoid becoming the Victim, a.k.a. loser, the first to have three defeats, while at the same time maneuvering to become the Survivor, the winner who ended up with the highest score after subtracting hazard cards from survivor cards.

To say Bill's luck was not the best tonight was an understatement. His first time around the board, he landed on Hazard and was sent to the Highway to a traffic accident and couldn't roll doubles after two tries in order to get away, and therefore collected his first defeat. Not only that, Brenda landed on that area and since he had no Survivor card to give her when she invaded, he had to take another Hazard card and was sent to the kitchen where a fire was raging. He sat there through two turns and again didn't roll doubles. The kitchen fire was his second defeat.

Polly and the other two women were happily speeding round the board collecting Survivor cards each time they passed Begin.

"Woo hoo!" Polly landed on the amusement park area where the outdoor card informed her she was having a wonderful day and won an extra Survivor card.

Brenda landed on the airplane area and the indoor card told her there was an accident. "Here's my survival card. No flight injury for me!"

"Wow! I'm set." When Dot landed on the bank area, the indoor card gave her three extra Survivor benefits.

The only indication of Bill's irritation was the tightening around his mouth, and Polly couldn't help but compare it to the way Walter would have pushed back from the table and stormed off. She found herself praying that Bill would land on the safety zone and thus have a respite from hazards for a while.

But the card fairy or whoever answers game prayers was not being gracious to Bill Trent. A hazard card sent him to the backyard area where he tripped over a stump but the only Survivor card in his possession was to save him from financial disaster.

He returned the salesman symbol to the box, stood up and grinned at the women. "Guess I'm just a natural victim tonight, huh?"

"Sorry." Polly shrugged. "Thanks for joining us."

The phone woke her up that Saturday morning and the clock showed that it was 9:30 a.m. She'd slept an hour past her usual wake up time, which was two hours past her arising time for the past forty years when she went out to a job.

Caller ID showed Sandy's number. Her best friend. Or used to be. To say that Sandy did not approve of the campground move was an enormous understatement. And Polly understood. They'd been brought up to think people who lived in trailers were, well, not quite...quite. And there was not much distinction between a trailer park and a campground, not when many people lived there year-round.

"Hey, miss you." The familiar voice sounded different from when she'd last heard it, the brittleness factor turned from potato chip to marshmallow.

Polly didn't even try to stop the sigh that slipped out from between her lips. "Same here."

"So, how are you getting along? Has the past week of being a permanent camper been as okay as the trial period?"

"Yes, definitely. Who would have ever guessed it? Sandy, I feel so free. It's like I have a brand-new start in a brand-new life and I love it." She quickly added, "I miss you, of course but everything else is wonderful. I can't explain it."

"Want company?"

"Are you serious?"

"Yes. I thought maybe I'd come down and spend a few days – see what has got you hooked."

"Oh, Sandy, that's great. When?"

"I was thinking maybe a week from Tuesday. And stay 'til Friday?"

"Can't you stay at least 'til Saturday? There's a Line Dancing party Friday night."

"Line dancing? You?"

Polly laughed. "Told you it's a brand-new life. Try it; you'll like it." She could almost see Sandy shaking her head with disbelief.

The two grew up in the Frankfort area, but their families were Country Club, not country music. They'd been friends since fifth grade, married partners in a law firm and lived in the same neighborhood in Louisville most of their adult life. Sandy, widowed three years ago, was still devastated over her loss. Polly, divorced a year, was not devastated at all. Sandy clung to the way things used to be while Polly put it all behind her.

"Jim's been bugging me to come and visit him, but I really don't want to stay there with his menagerie." Jim was Sandy's only sibling who had been like a little brother to Polly too. She hadn't seen him for years. She and Walter were in England at the time Sandy's husband died, so they didn't even get back for the funeral. Jim was also divorced, had been for a long time, and was reportedly happy as the local sheriff.

"Menagerie?"

"Yes! He has two dogs, a cat, an aquarium, and miniature frogs. Just the idea of those frogs getting loose and jumping in bed with me gives me the creeps."

Polly laughed. That was one thing she and Sandy had in common. They were not pet people.

Sandy's voice went from marshmallow to honey. "Forgive me?"

Polly swallowed hard. "Already a done deal."

"I love you!"

"I love you too. Friends forever." The words they used at age eleven when they took a pin and drew blood from their pointer fingers and held them together.

"Friends forever," Sandy echoed. "See you in ten days. I'll call with details later."

Chapter Five

Jim looked over the list that Saturday and chose the Hollands, who lived next door to Angie Lee. Two women with the same last name. He'd bet they knew everything that went on in Windy Hills.

He knocked at the door and it was opened before he could take his hand away. They must have seen the car pull up out front.

"Come in." The little gray-haired lady had a strong grip as she took hold of his wrist and pulled him in. A taller woman stood behind her and echoed her greeting.

"Ladies, I'm Sheriff Jim Murray."

"Yes, Your Honor." The shorter of the two nodded. "We've been expecting you. Your henchman was here earlier and told us what's happened." She looked over at her sister with arched brows. "Not that we were surprised.

They led him into the living room and indicated the middle cushion on a plush sofa. As soon as he was seated, one sister perched on each side and turned toward him, eagerness evident in every gesture.

The room was such a shock that he was momentarily speechless. There were two sofas, each with little doily things on the back above every cushion. And there were three wingback chairs also adorned with the lacy things. With the exception of the couch they were occupying and the pathway they walked to get there, every available inch of space on the floor and furnishings was filled with dolls. Some were three or four feet in height and some were miniatures. There were some baby dolls and a few Barbie dolls. Most were replicas of adult women dressed in costumes of other centuries.

He brought his attention back to the reason he came. "You weren't surprised? At the murder?"

"Not a bit. We knew it was just a matter of time."

"Just a matter of time." The taller sister repeated.

"Well, ladies. It seems you have a lot to tell me." He started to sit back and then remembered the lacy things.

"It's quite all right to lean back, your Honor. We have tatted antimacassars to save the upholstery."

"Tell him, Minnie." The taller one nodded.

"He wouldn't be interested in that, Kate."

"What? I'm interested in everything." He was starting to get dizzy turning from one to the other.

"Well, do you know why these are called antimacassars?"

"No, Ma'am." He'd thought they were called doilies.

"Because gentlemen used to wear a brand of hair oil called Macasser's."

The taller one giggled.

"And the oil left terrible marks on the cloth of

chairs and sofas, so ..." She paused dramatically.

He laughed. "I see...anti – Macasser's."

"Exactly!" Both ladies tittered with laughter.

If he didn't get them back on track, he could be here all day. "Well now, you've taught me something. And what else did you want to tell me?"

"Tell him, Minnie."

The smaller sister sighed. "This is unpleasant and we're not ones to gossip. If a crime had not been committed, this information would have never left our lips."

The taller one nodded.

"You see, we don't always sleep well. Sometimes we wake up in the middle of the night."

"In the middle of the night," came the echo.

"And we see things. We see people. We've seen our next-door neighbor walking at very strange hours."

"Very strange hours."

"And sometimes we've gone walking too." Miss Minnie paused. "We've seen what goes on at the swimming pool. For months now."

"Yes?" He looked from one sister to the other. "What goes on?"

"Wickedness." Miss Kate surprised him by speaking first. "Carnal wickedness." She said it with relish and Jim stifled a smile before it reached his lips.

Miss Minnie took up the explanation. "Angela Lee meets Mr. Adams at the pool most every night."

"They do it in the water!" Miss Kate blurted it out as if she was amazed at the feat.

Jim scratched the top of his nose with fingertips, allowing the palm of his hand to cover his mouth.

"Ah, that explains how he got in there. She has a

key." He turned to Miss Minnie. "Did you see them last night?"

She looked disappointed. "No. We slept well last night."

When he finally concluded the sisters had told him everything they knew, he bid them good-bye.

"Come again, your Honor. Anytime." They stood at the door waving until he drove away.

At last he could laugh out loud. 'Your Honor.' Judge Simmons would love that!

Next, he drove back toward the main entrance and up into the clubhouse driveway. He pulled into the parking lot and got out of the car. The clubhouse sat on a small hill and could be seen from the entire subdivision. Anyone up here could see out over Windy Hills Estates as well as spot an approaching car. He walked around to the side nearest the entrance road. The windows had blinds over them, but he'd find out if Will Coates would be able to see out of them while watching movies during the night. If that was where the equipment was, it would be a perfect spot for a guard when he wasn't patrolling.

He drove down the hill and crossed the entrance road into the driveway of the large house there. The biggest home in the estates belonged to Sydney and Margaret White.

Margaret White was a dignified looking woman in her fifties, salt and pepper hair, soft spoken. She invited him in and asked if he would like a cup of coffee. He declined, figuring she might dump it on his head when he brought up what he came about.

"Ma'am, this is unpleasant, but I have to talk to you."

She nodded. "I understand, Sheriff. Your deputy came by to tell me the news yesterday. He said you'd be questioning everyone."

"Yes, Ma'am. But this is more personal."

She took a deep breath. "You found out about my affair with Paul Adams?"

"Yes, Ma'am." Jim also took a deep breath. That was easier than he anticipated.

"I suppose it was Stephanie who told you." There was a slight question at the end of her statement but when he didn't answer she continued. "It ended almost as soon as it began. It's been over fourteen years since that happened. Did she tell you about catching us?"

"No, Ma'am."

"We met at the clubhouse a few times, in the middle of the night. And one night when Stephanie was sleeping over at our house, the two girls sneaked out, got our key from the hook and – well, you can imagine the rest." The lines in her face became more pronounced. "It was a nightmare. Paul and I didn't know then who it was, just that someone unlocked the door and opened it. By the time we jumped up from the couch, the door slammed shut and whoever entered was gone. Later Melanie, that's my daughter, confessed it was them. I promised her it would never happen again. And it hasn't."

She was very quiet – and believable. Very much a lady.

"I'm not proud of that, Sheriff. Not proud of my actions. And not proud of being one of the long line of woman with whom Paul Adams betrayed Susan."

Ah! "There were others?"

"Always. We all went to high school together. Even

then, although Paul and Susan were going steady, he would sneak off with other girls." She gave a short laugh. "But he was good. He could convince you that you were the one – the female for whom he would give up all others. He convinced Susan, when we all knew he only married her for her money. And later he convinced me, for a short time."

"She has money?"

"A lot of money. That's how he was able to start the insurance business."

"Mrs. White. I have to ask this. Did your husband know about your affair with Mr. Adams?"

She laughed again, this time with sarcasm. "You mean would he have killed him in a jealous rage fourteen years later? No, Sheriff. Not only did Sydney not know about it, he wouldn't have cared if he did. Why do you think I was such a perfect target for Paul?"

He didn't answer and she continued. "Sydney isn't like Paul, not just in it for the game. His problem is that he needs young beautiful women to make him feel young and good about himself. I used to be young and beautiful." She said it with a quiet dignity and Jim believed her.

It was after one when he pulled out of the White's driveway, so he turned the car toward town and lunch. Maybe Wendy's today. He went inside and after getting his burger and fries, took the tray to a table. There weren't many people at this hour and it was a quiet atmosphere to think about the new information he had.

Paul Adams was a real ladies man, had a short affair with Mrs. White, and was in the middle of a longer one with Angie Lee when his death put an end to it.

Margaret White said her husband wouldn't have cared about her having an affair with Paul Adams. But he liked younger women. What if Paul Adams had taken Angie Lee away from Sydney White? Could that have been a motive for the murder? White had a pool key. After he ate he'd go talk to Angie Lee again.

Just as he was emptying the contents of the tray into the trash container, his cell phone rang. It was Stephanie Adams. She sounded near hysteria and asked him to come to the house right away.

He pulled up to the curb and she opened the front door before he got out of the car.

She wasn't crying but she sure looked upset. She led him down the hall and into a bedroom. "This is my Mother's room."

He looked around. But didn't see anything out of place. He looked over to the place where Stephanie nodded her head. A large stack of greeting cards and a key lay on an old-fashioned dressing table with a frilly skirt.

"I found these," she said. "She's at the beauty shop and I knew it would be the perfect time to look for evidence."

Odd. Did she want her mother to be guilty? He walked over to the table and picked up the stack. They were all romantic cards. And all were signed Stevie. He laid them down again and turned around to look at Stephanie.

"My mother is insane."

"What do you mean? Because she kept cards? From your father?"

Stephanie shook her head. "These aren't from my father. It's her handwriting. She writes them to herself.

And look at the key. I bet it's the key to the pool area across the street."

He pulled a key ring from his pocket and sorted through 'til he found the one marked WA Pool. He picked up the key from the dressing table. An exact match.

"I knew it." Stephanie's head dropped against his shoulder and her hands grabbed his arm. "I've been afraid of this ever since I got the call."

"Afraid of what?" He wanted her to say it instead of him.

"Afraid that it was my mother who killed my father." The tears came then.

He turned and put his arms around her and she sobbed into his chest. When the crying subsided, she pulled back and grabbed a tissue from her mother's dressing table.

"I guess you'll want to take the knives with you."

"Yes, I was thinking that." He called and asked Tony Morales to bring some evidence bags. By two thirty when Susan Adams phoned from the beauty shop for a ride home, the knives were with the deputy on the way to the lab.

"I hate to leave you alone with her," Jim said, looking at the grief-stricken blonde. "But I can't make an arrest without more evidence than possession of a key. Why do you think she did it? You said she didn't have any emotion, so jealousy wouldn't be the motive."

She dropped her head for a minute and then lifted it and nodded. "Remember, I said that I was flying in next week?"

"Yes."

"Dad was going to have her committed to a mental

institution. He wanted me here for that. She must have found out."

That made sense. But how did she get the key?

Stephanie refused to go to a motel for the night, saying she would be safe. After extracting her promise to call his cell phone anytime and also to lock her bedroom door that night, Jim left and drove a block to the Lee house.

Angie Lee looked a hundred per cent better today. She wasn't as attractive as he'd first thought but maybe that was because Stephanie Adams made her fade into the background of his mind.

Angie wasn't happy when he confronted her with the news that she and Paul Adams had been seen together afterhours at the pool for months.

"Caught, huh?" She gave a little grimace. "I didn't kill him."

"No, I don't believe you did. Why would you?"

Her eyes widened. "Right. But how do you know I wouldn't?"

He wasn't about to divulge his recent discovery about the victim's wife. "What I need from you...again..." He gave her a stern look. "Is to know how many keys to the pool gate there are."

She sighed. "Just one more than I told you. Paul wanted one, so he could get in and leave without being dependent on me. He liked to relax alone after...well, you know."

"Did he always stay alone afterwards?"

She nodded.

"And you didn't lock the gate when you left?"

"No, that way if Will Coates or anyone came by, Paul could say he found the gate open."

"But surely Coates would remember locking it earlier."

She emitted a snort of laughter. "Will Coates skips so many of his designated assignments, he wouldn't remember what he'd done when."

"Do you know if he vacuums the pool every morning?"

A half smile sprang to her lips. "Yes, no."

He stared at her. "Huh?"

"Yes, I know, and the answer is no. Actually, he does a bunch of stuff with the pool on Monday after the heavy use on weekends. And he vacuums on Wednesday and Friday. So, it's every other day, except on weekends. Pretty much everybody knows that."

"One more question, Mrs. Lee. Did you have an affair with Sydney White prior to your relationship with Paul Adams?"

Her nostrils flared. "What does that have to do with anything?"

"Motives, Ma'am. If Mr. White was jealous..."

She shrugged. "Could be."

"And who hates you?"

"What do you mean?"

"They chose a Tuesday, when they knew you'd be the one to find the body."

Monday morning. Paul's funeral was scheduled for tomorrow. Susan rolled over in bed and the book she'd been reading when she fell asleep dropped to the floor. No odor of coffee greeted her nostrils and the clock showed that it was nearly ten o' clock. She jumped out of bed. Stephanie would fuss at her for laziness.

She was in the shower when her daughter's voice came from the adjoining bedroom. "Mother, Sheriff Murray is here again. So come to the living room when you get out."

Here again? Why? A vague uneasiness tightened her stomach. But maybe that was just hunger.

After she was dry she went to the closet and chose her clothes for the day. White slacks and a blue top with the white sandals. That would do. By the time she was dressed the curling iron was hot.

It was only twenty-five minutes from the time Stephanie called until she entered the living room. Hopefully it was quick enough to avoid a scene.

When she entered she saw the Sheriff and the lady police officer. They both stood up. Stephanie was watching her intently from Paul's favorite chair. The look on her daughter's face sent a chill of alarm through her body.

The sheriff held up a paper. "Mrs. Adams. I have here a warrant for your arrest for the murder of your husband. You have the right to remain silent..."

How could this be happening? She looked over at her daughter. And knew.

When Susan Adams was safely locked in a cell at the county detention center, Jim took Helen Bailey to lunch.

"She'll be out on bail within hours." He chomped down on his Wendy's double with everything. Small town, good family. It was a given.

"I'd hate to see your cholesterol count." Helen was eating a salad and plain baked potato. She didn't wait for him to respond. "I'm just not sure she did it."

He paused mid chomp. "What? But the butcher knife from her kitchen had traces of blood – same type as her husband, same as on the lounge chair. And she had the pool key where she'd locked back up after she killed him."

"It just doesn't feel right to me." She paused as if weighing her words. "I don't like the daughter."

He started to say that she was just jealous, but the words stopped at his tongue. Jealous? A whole new thought came to his mind. Could Helen Bailey be jealous because he was attracted to Stephanie? Surely not. "Why don't you like her?"

"I'm not sure, Jim." She frowned. "There's just something about her."

"Woman's intuition?"

"No. But I've been thinking what she said about her mother's not having any emotion. That just doesn't match up with all the romance books. It seems to me more like her emotions are repressed, that she's living vicariously through books."

He grinned. "And what TV programs have you been watching, Dr. Bailey?"

A blush sprang up in her cheeks. "Sorry. I guess I'm just sorry for Mrs. Adams. Her husband sounds like a scum and her daughter doesn't seem to care about her either." She halfheartedly took a bite of her salad. "Do you mind if I check into some things?"

He wiped the last remnant of the burger from his lips. "Not at all."

Jim was at the other side of the county all afternoon checking out a report of vandalism on sixty acres of undeveloped property. It looked like someone – he figured kids - had tried to develop it into something slightly less than a commune, cooking over open fires, smoking pot, drinking beer. Slightly less only because they weren't actually sleeping there. When he returned to the office, he found that just as he predicted Susan Adams was no longer at the detention center. The only thing that surprised him was that they reported Officer Helen Bailey was the one who picked her up.

But maybe not so surprising when he thought back on their conversation at lunch.

Helen was a nice woman. He was kind of sorry himself that Mrs. Adams was the killer. He'd rather it have been Sydney White. He remembered the thought that came to his mind as they sat at Wendy's. Maybe Helen was interested in him?

He shook his head. Nah.

He sure would like to see Stephanie again. But his business in Windy Acres was over. You didn't go make a social call to a house where you'd arrested the owner hours earlier. But he could call.

Stephanie answered her cell phone after the second ring. "Hello, Sheriff." Her voice was warm and inviting. And she'd recognized his number on her caller id.

"I just wanted to see if you're okay. I heard your mother is out on bail."

"Yes. And I'll be fine. She doesn't seem upset at all. And I don't think she suspects that I was the one who went through her dresser."

"Where is she now?"

"In her room. Reading."

He took a deep breath. "If you decide you'd like to get out, and want company, call me."

"You are so kind, Jim. You don't mind if I call you Jim do you, Sheriff Murray?"

"Not at all." Boy, did he ever not mind!

But by the time he fell asleep watching television, she hadn't called.

The parking lot at Rogers that Tuesday was filled with cars. The visitation began at noon and the funeral service was scheduled for two.

It was one forty-five when he entered the mortuary. He was surprised to see Officer Bailey sitting on the front row with Mrs. Adams. Stephanie was standing by the closed casket talking to a small group of people. She looked sharp in a dark blue suit, her long blonde hair curling slightly on her shoulders.

He wanted to go up and speak to her but felt awkward since her mother was so close by. Just then she looked toward the back and saw him...and smiled. Did her eyes hold a look of longing that matched his own?

He wondered if she'd call tonight. And how long she'd be in town. Maybe she'd move back. That was a cheering thought. Maybe she'd keep his mind off of the impossible thing he'd always wanted. Or even destroy it.

He looked around at the crowd. The Holland sisters were there and Sydney and Margaret White. Angie Lee was conspicuously absent.

At noon on Wednesday his phone rang. The display showed Helen's number.

"I hate to tell you this, Romeo, but you need to get your handcuffs out again."

"What do you mean?"

"Well, remember you said I could check out some things?"

"Yes. What did you find out?"

"That Stephanie Adams flew in on Monday night instead of Tuesday."

"What?"

"Yep, she must have been in Lexington when her mother called her cell phone to tell her about the murder." She paused for a minute. "Of course, she already knew about it."

"Now, wait a minute. You don't know that. She might have had some other reason for being in Kentucky." His mind was whirling. "And after finding out about the murder, she wouldn't want to admit that and make herself a suspect."

"I just got the lab report from the hot tea she made for her mother Thursday night."

"What?"

"I told Susan not to eat or drink anything she didn't fix herself. She did as I asked and poured the tea into a jar. It was full of digitalis. A lethal dose."

"Digitalis?"

"Paul Adams took it for his heart. I guess it was handy for Stephanie to use."

"But why?"

"I don't know. You can ask her. I'll meet you there."

The four of them were once again seated in the Adams living room.

"My father never realized how much talent I have. But when I graduated college, he helped me financially for five years, so I could get established in Hollywood." She shook her head. "I recently met some important people and know this is the breakthrough I've been waiting for. But he wouldn't listen and refused to send any more money. I came in last month to beg him. But..." Her mouth formed a sneer. "That's when I found out about his nightly pool rendezvous. He bought the ticket for me to come home next week and said that was the last cent he'd spend on me in California. But I didn't want to come home." She looked at Jim as if inviting his understanding. "It's my lifelong dream.

"Mother's so unhappy with life anyway, nothing much matters to her. So I thought it all out and made my plan." She laughed. "What's one more plane ticket on my credit card? Besides I figured after he was gone, I'd have all the money I need to pay it off."

Jim watched her with growing horror. He'd been attracted to this monster?

"I bought the butcher knife after I landed in Lexington. And rented a car. Tuesday night I drove down here, pulled off the side of the road and under some trees, and walked into Windy Acres. Just in case the guard happened to be watching the entrance." Her voice dripped sarcasm.

"When my father's latest plaything left, I slipped up behind him and ... well, you know. It was easy. He'd been drinking and didn't even try to fight. I dumped him into the pool and left. Simple." She smiled proudly at Jim and Helen.

"I took his key – he left it on the table while he was there and then locked up when he decided to go home. I put the knife in a plastic bag and brought it home with me the next day." She looked at her mother. "I didn't put it in the kitchen drawer 'til you were at the beauty shop that afternoon. The same time I put the key with your cards." The disgust in her voice was obvious.

Jim looked over at Susan Adams whose face was concealed by her hands.

"I found those cards when I was in last month too." She shook her head. "Stevie! Is he a phantom lover? Somebody from those silly romantic novels you read all the time?"

Susan looked up and her lips tightened before she spoke. "Stevie was what I called your father when we were in high school. Back when he loved me. I...I pretended he still does. Still did." She drew in a deep breath and released it before she held her hand out to Helen Bailey, who took it.

Stephanie opened her purse and pulled out a sheet of paper. "Dad had a full bottle of digitalis and it was easy to put it into the nightly tea. I learned to imitate her handwriting when I was in school." She turned to her mother and smiled sarcastically. "You always gave me permission for anything I wanted to do." She handed the paper to Jim.

He read aloud. "I killed my husband because I heard him tell my daughter he was going to have me committed to a mental institution. I don't want to live in any institution including a prison. So this is the best way out for me." It was signed Susan Adams.

That night as they sat at Wendy's, Jim only picked at his food.

"That was a shock. You're good, Helen." It was hard to admit it, but he had to be fair.

"I know it." She grinned at him. Then the smile left her face. "Poor lady. She was embarrassed that we found out about the cards she left herself every night. She still loves that boy from high school."

Jim snorted. "From the information I got, he was cheating on her then...married her for her money. Guess his daughter inherited the 'do anything for money' gene. I thought it was a crime of passion and it turns out to be just money." He sighed and shrugged his shoulders.

"One of these days I'm going to commit a crime of passion!" Helen had a strange look on her face.

"What do you mean?"

"Sheriff, you need another full-time deputy. Badly."

She stood up, leaned over the table, kissed him on the lips, and walked out the door.

Chapter Six

Polly smiled. Her best friend would be there in only three days. She put her cell phone on the bedside table and was just reaching in the closet for a pair of slacks when the shrill sound of a siren filled the air. Peeking out the bedroom window, she saw a blue light flashing on a car that turned in and came to a screeching halt at the office.

She dressed hurriedly, ignoring make up and giving her teeth a quick brushing. Within five minutes she was near the office. A crowd had gathered several sites away at Tom Broughton's trailer. The door was open and evidently the police officer was inside. Polly edged up to Brenda.

"What's going on?"

Brenda shook her head. "It's Tom. He's dead!"

"What?" Polly couldn't believe she'd heard right. Brenda nodded. "Dot's hysterical. Tom didn't show up at the office so one of the campers got her to open up, so they could buy some bait. Then she went to his camper and there was no answer. She got her key, went in, and found him dead."

Polly's right hand went automatically to her throat in an instinctive desire to aid in dissipating the lump that formed there. "Dead?"

Brenda nodded. "Not just dead. Murdered."

"Dot's in there with the sheriff." June Gabbard whispered to Brenda loud enough for Polly to hear.

Polly looked at the car with the blue flashing light. It was white and announced that it belonged to the Franklin County Sheriff. Jim? Or maybe it would be a deputy. It was the weekend. Maybe a head sheriff, or whatever he was, got weekends off.

In a very few minutes, the door to the camper opened and a man walked down the steps; it was definitely her friend's younger brother who immediately turned and gave his hand to Dot Broughton to help her descend. Dot had several tissues held to her face and it was obvious that she had been crying.

What a horrible situation. Polly couldn't imagine finding Walter's dead body, even if he had betrayed and belittled her most of her life. Even if she didn't love him anymore. And she didn't think ... well, maybe Dot did still love Tom. It was obvious last night she was at least a little jealous of Jill Trent.

Brenda said he was murdered. How? She'd ask as soon as Jim and Dot passed through the crowd. Jim Murray. How long had it been? Twenty, thirty years? More?

Just as he ushered the weeping Dot past them, he looked over at Polly and let a tiny twinkle of recognition fill his eyes and a smile touch his lips.

Wow! Polly's stomach reacted in a way that shocked her. Little brother had definitely improved with age! He'd be fifty-nine now. There was some gray at his temples, but the wavy dark brown hair was still thick, and the chestnut colored eyes still hinted of that sense of humor that he used to drive her and his sister crazy when they were kids.

It didn't take long to make up her mind that she would stay outside and hang around the office 'til she could say hello ... ah! she could offer to run the office. She quickly followed the two walking away.

"Dot?" They both stopped and turned around at her call. Polly nodded to Jim to let him know that she recognized him too, and then she spoke to the grief-stricken woman. "Dot, I'd be happy to handle the office for you so you can just go rest and contact family and all that."

Dot took a deep breath that Polly interpreted as a sigh of relief. She reached in her pocket and withdrew a key which she handed to Polly. "Thank you."

"You are very welcome." Polly hugged the other woman before she took the key from her hand. Jim continued to guide Dot down the sloping drive to her camper. Since the patrol car was still parked in front of the office, Polly knew she would see Jim again before he left.

The people who swarmed into the office didn't seem to be enthusiastic about their purchases but used that as an excuse to question her about the manager's death. Polly could honestly say that she didn't know any more than they did, that Tom Broughton was found dead by his ex-wife Dot. How he died was a mystery to her. Yes, she heard it was murder but didn't even know why that rumor got started. For all she knew, he could have peacefully passed away in his sleep.

Finally, the door opened and Jim Murray walked in. The office got very quiet and the customers paid for their goods and left. Polly noticed through the window that they all gathered at the shelter house across the street instead of going back to their campers.

Jim grinned, that mischievous boy grin of his that took her back over five decades.

"Hey, Other Big Sis. I'd hug you, but I imagine we're under surveillance - wouldn't want to hurt your reputation."

Polly found herself wishing she was swept up in those strong arms. What on earth was going on? She laughed nervously.

"Surely they wouldn't think anything about an older woman being hugged by her young brother, faux though he may be."

"Hey, at our age, what's three years? And by the way, you look great. I imagine if anyone was guessing, they'd think I was the older one."

"Flatterer!" She grinned back at him.

He looked out the window toward the shelter. "If you don't mind, I'd just as soon no one knew about our connection."

That was a surprise!

"Why not?"

Jim frowned. "Not sure. Just a gut thing. Wouldn't want anybody seeing you as on the other side. Lots of times in situations like this, law enforcement becomes if not the enemy, at least a hindrance to normal life."

Polly nodded. "Gotcha. Can I ask how Tom Broughton died?"

"Don't see why not. The coroner is on his way, but
it looks like he died from a blow to the forehead."

She nodded. "So it was murder, like they said!" She
shook her head and then remembered. "Jim, did you
know Sandy is coming down Tuesday?"

He frowned. "Really? I've been trying to get her to
come stay with me."

Polly didn't want to mention the dreaded menagerie. "We planned it last week. I begged her. I mean I love
it here, but I really miss your sister."

The wrinkles left his forehead. "Yeah, me too. She
told me about your move. Now that you're here maybe
I'll see her more often."

Just then a car drove up out front. The Coroner
had arrived. An ambulance followed shortly.

When the body had been removed from the camper
and driven away, Jim Murray came back into the office.

"Where would be the best place for me to interview
the, uh, are they residents or visitors, or what?"

"Some of both," Polly told him. She pointed to the
shelter. "I think that might be your best bet. I can use
the loud speaker and announce that the shelter house
will be unavailable for games and fellowship until the
sheriff is through talking to us individually."

He nodded. "Sounds good. And how do I get them
to come? Go from camper to camper?"

"I'll make a list of residents and weekenders if you
want and the campsite addresses."

"I'll call for some help from the city police and they
can go knock on doors and bring them to be inter-

viewed." He pulled out his cell phone.

After he hung up, they reminisced about high school days. Polly was still shocked at her reaction to the man she'd always thought of as Sandy's little brother. Wow. She hadn't had this kind of reaction in, well, had she ever?

Within twenty minutes, Officer Helen Bailey joined them in the office. She looked to be in her late thirties, and really cute. Small with a good figure. Not what Polly expected in a police officer.

Jim introduced them and Polly handed her the list and went to the microphone to make the announcement. The campers who were still at the shelter house put their cards away and vacated immediately. Jim walked over to the shelter and Officer Bailey took the list and headed to the lower campground. Jim had told her to begin with the residents, the owners of RiversEdge, most of whom lived in that section. Newcomers, within the past five years, were in the upper campground, with the exception of the manager.

Polly would have loved to be a fly on the wall and hear what her neighbors had to say. That desire reminded her how she and Sandy used to want to be like Nancy Drew or Judy Bolton.

Hmmm. She pulled her cell phone from her pocket.

Sandy answered immediately.

"Do you have to wait 'til Tuesday to come down?"

"Well, not really but if you want me to stay through next Friday night, it would be an awfully long visit."

"Well, guess who's here and what's happened?"

When they hung up ten minutes later, Sandy had promised to be there by suppertime.

It was one o'clock when Polly realized that Jim and

his deputy were probably hungry.

As soon as the Colonel, the latest one being inter-
viewed, left and before the deputy could bring in
someone else, Polly joined them in the shelter house
and offered to fix them some lunch.

Jim stretched and looked at his watch. "It is that
time isn't it? Helen?" He looked at his assistant.

She shook her head. "Not me. I had a power drink
on the way out."

Polly resisted the urge to stick her tongue out and
say "Blech!" And then inwardly shook herself. What's
wrong, old lady? Jealous of the young, slim girl? No, of
course not.

"Well, I'm ready to take a break."

"You're both welcome to come to my camper and
I'll fix you a sandwich. I can get my friend Brenda to
watch the office."

Helen Bailey shook her head. "I'd like to go wander
around down by the river if that's okay?" She looked at
the sheriff.

He nodded. "That's fine. We'll be in ... " He turned
to Polly. "Which site is yours?"

"Site 46," she pointed down the row of campers behind the shelter house.

Jim nodded and turned to his deputy. "I'll call your
cell if I'm through before you come back."

As Polly closed the door to her camper behind
them, she hesitated. "Do you think it might blow the
cover off our relationship for you to come here for
lunch? I didn't think about that when I invited you."

Jim was looking around the camper and nodding
in obvious admiration. "Nice. No, we'll just say I was
going to interview you next and you took pity on my

stomach, so we did the interviewing here."

"Without your deputy present?"

"You've got a point, but we'll just say she didn't want lunch and would join us for the questioning. That's the truth."

Polly nodded. "If you say so. It's your ball game." She opened the refrigerator. "You have a choice. Warmed over Chicken Alfredo with peppers, onions, and mushrooms or a corned beef sandwich. Both with a tossed salad and homemade bleu cheese dressing."

Jim smiled. "The Alfredo sounds great! And I love bleu cheese dressing."

Polly hoped her smile didn't show the triumph she felt. Walter hated Northern Italian and only used ranch dressing.

She pointed him to the table, which sat back in the slideout, the camper version of a bay window and one of her favorite parts of her new home. When they were both seated, Jim shocked her by taking her hand and asking permission to say the blessing.

"Why, of course. I'd love for you to."

And he did.

There was silence for about five minutes while he wolfed down the Alfredo like he hadn't eaten in days. He stopped halfway through and ate the salad.

"This is great! When did you turn into such a good cook?"

"Just always loved it. Walter's mother really taught me how to cook. At first. Then I started experimenting and trying to copy things I ate at restaurants. And I found that lots of the time my recipes turned out better than the ones I was copying. Like fried chicken tenders, stir fried spinach, mushrooms over Italian bread, and ... " She laughed. "Listen to me, bragging. But I do love to cook."

"And you are great at it. When this mess is over, why don't you invite me out for all that stuff you just said."

"Deal!"

When he had finished the last bite of seconds, he wiped his mouth with the napkin, picked up his plate and salad bowl, put them in the sink, and rinsed them off.

"Why thank you! I wasn't expecting that."

His smile made her stomach do funny things again. "I've grown up and gotten better manners than when you were around me most." He sat back down at the table.

She felt silly, but her eyes filled with tears. "Lot of water under the bridge, huh?"

"Did you know I was madly in love with you when you were in high school and I was in junior high?"

"No!"

"Yeah, to you I was just Sandy's little pest brother. But to me you were the most beautiful, exciting, and kind person in the world."

She remembered that Sandy treated him pretty bad and she had often taken up for him. But then there were the other times.

"But I've felt so guilty about the cowboy soda."

Jim threw back his head and whooped with laughter. "Yeah that was pretty lame. I blamed it on Sandy and conveniently refused to acknowledge your participation."

The girls had found a cup that looked like a cowboy boot, took white lotion that smelled like almonds, mixed it with baby powder and some of Mrs. Murray's perfume and filled the cup. They handed it to Jim as a treat they'd made for him. A Cowboy Soda. The horrified look on young Jim's face when he gulped down that first - and last - drink of the concoction was one of Polly's most vivid, and guilt producing, memories.

"I'm so sorry. I'm not so sure it wasn't my idea. Forgive me?"

"Of course. Even back then I wished you were my big sister."

"Love is blind." Then she could feel her cheeks turning red. Why? They were talking about sibling type love. But he'd said that later he loved her in a different way.

Jim straightened up in the chair and pulled out a notebook and pen. "Okay, nostalgia time is over. It's down to business."

He'd already been told about the dog kicking incident. And she felt like a gossip but knew she had to tell him about the manager's flirtation with Jill Trent.

It was after he left her camper that she realized she hadn't told him about his sister's change of plans. But the hug he gave her before he opened the door drove everything else out of her mind.

"He thinks of you as an older sister," she reminded herself.

"But there was a time that he thought of you as the most beautiful person in the world," herself replied.

"But that was almost 50 years ago."

"So? And at your time of life, three years age difference doesn't mean a thing."

"Oh stop it! There is a man who is dead, at least one person grieving, and a murderer somewhere here in RiversEdge Campground! This is no time to get into romantic daydreams. And about somebody you've always thought of as a younger brother!"

Chapter Seven

He left the campground but didn't make it back to the office before another tragedy happened. The tires screeched when he turned the squad car, not exactly on a dime but close. Stupid teens. Not only putting their own lives in danger but everybody else's too, including his. The guys in back of the pickup must have realized they'd been spotted and alerted the driver because the truck disappeared into an alley with a screeching of tires similar to his own.

But he'd outsmart 'em. Passing the alley entrance he turned left at the next intersection and turned on lights and siren. He also called the police station. After all it was their jurisdiction.

He just hoped they had a cruiser close by. But he had a sneaking suspicion the kids were headed out into his territory. Probably the same gang that hung out sometimes on the deserted property a couple of miles outside of town off '127. Somebody complained a month or so ago that there was a commune there and he'd checked it out. But it wasn't a commune, just the remains of a lot of parties – beer bottles, cigarette and marijuana stubs. He'd stopped by a few times after that on Friday or Saturday nights but there'd been no sign of further activity and he hadn't thought much about it again. Until he saw the truckload of kids.

By the time he traveled the two blocks that let him turn left onto Harrison, there was a city car coming from the other direction, also with lights and siren. The pickup was just getting ready to turn left out of the alley when the driver must have realized that he was caught in either direction because he stopped. Jim hoped the kid wasn't stupid enough to try to back down the alleyway. But the hope died as the front end disappeared from sight.

Without a word of planned cooperation, the city car made a right and Jim turned into the alley. He knew the one-way street on the other side would let the police block the truck from that end. And he had it covered from this one.

The driver of the pickup must have spotted them both again because he slammed on the brakes and stopped. It would have been perfect if a kid in the truck bed behind the passenger seat hadn't tumbled out of the truck and landed on his head.

Jim leaped out of the car and ran to kneel beside the boy. Out of the corner of his eye, he caught a glimpse of a city uniform standing over them. No pulse. Must have broken his neck. Damn!

He glanced up at the other officer to shake his head and convey the news. His stomach tightened even further when he saw it was Sgt. Helen Bailey. The eyes that met his were watering up. She probably was thinking the same thing he was. If they hadn't chased the kids, this boy would still be alive.

The driver and his buddy in the passenger seat were taken into police headquarters and questioned. The guys in the truck bed had jumped off the other side and disappeared while Jim and Helen were with the body of Jerry Andrews, calling the ambulance, reporting to police headquarters. They hadn't said a word to each other. After that first look, they hadn't even glanced at one another.

When the driver had been booked and taken off to a cell, Jim asked the passenger if he wanted a ride home. The kid just nodded.

"I'm sorry about your friend," Jim said as they drove away from the station. "It was what we were trying to prevent, you know. It's dangerous. And illegal. To ride in an open truck bed. And your driver friend was speeding, too."

The kid, Billy McAlpin, nodded but didn't say anything. When they got to his house, Billy's Mom was standing inside the storm door. She flung it open and ran down the sidewalk toward the squad car before Jim could even park it.

Wow. The kid was good looking but couldn't compare to the mother. Blonde. Well, except for a half inch at the roots. Great body. The shorts and lowcut top left no doubt about that.

What was wrong with him? A friend of her fifteen-year-old son's has died. Her son taken to the police station and released only because he and the driver both swore that he'd begged to stop and let the sheriff warn them or whatever he was going to do. A worried mother, even now embracing her son like there was no tomorrow. And here he was giving her the twice over. Man! Was this a deep seated emotional "I don't care" reaction to seeing Polly again? She obviously still thought of him as a younger brother.

Jim got out and walked around the car to where the two stood in a silent embrace. He could see the woman whispering in her son's ear. When she looked up, her eyes narrowed. "Are you satisfied, Sheriff? Did you get your man?"

He shook his head. "Ma'am, I can't tell you how sorry I am. But we were trying to prevent somebody getting hurt. Your son understood that."

Mrs. McAlpin looked back at her son and her face softened.

She was pretty too.

"I'll be going now. I'm glad you were inside the truck, Billy. I'm glad you weren't hurt."

Billy just nodded, then turned toward the house and walked inside. His mother watched him before she turned to Jim. "I'm sorry, Sheriff. I really do understand. It's just..." Her face crumpled into a mask of sorrow, and tears began to flow. The next thing Jim knew she was in his arms, crying on his shoulder. He didn't mind holding her at all but feared an irate husband charging out the door at any second.

"...no father since he was seven," she was saying. "I try but I just can't do it all." She sobbed harder. "He got in with the wrong crowd." She pulled back slightly and wiped away tears with the back of her hand. When she looked up at him with eyes the color of violets, he felt his stomach turn over. He gently pushed himself away from her. Unwillingly, but it was the right thing to do.

"I'm so sorry. If there is anything I can do..."

"Yes, there is, Sheriff." Her hand reached out and clutched his arm. "You could spend time with Billy. He needs the influence of a good man."

Jim swallowed. "I'll think about it, Mrs. McAlpin." He ought to get in the car and leave. But her hand was still on his arm and he couldn't be rude, could he?

Her lips began to curl into a slight smile. "Thank you so much. And please call me Patsy. I hope..." She stared into his eyes again with an intensity that made him dizzy. "I hope we'll become friends." Then she removed her hand. "Thank you for bringing Billy home." She nodded and walked into the house without a backward glance.

When she closed the door, Jim turned back to the car, got in, and drove away.

Deputies Hank Mills and Tony Morales were both in the office when he entered to make his own report.

"What're you doing here?" Jim looked at Tony. Hank answered.

"Helen called and told me what happened. I thought maybe you might want to take off after your report. So I phoned Tony."

"Helen, huh? What business is it of hers?" Jim knew he was being unfair but Helen Bailey could get on his very last nerve. He never could figure out her motives, or even the meaning of her actions. He shook his head to dislodge the scene at Wendy's when she'd reached across the table and kissed him – on the mouth!

Hank grinned. "You know, I think she's got it for you, boss."

Morales added his own grin. "Can't see what she sees in you but..."

"Okay, guys. Cut the crap. I've got to get busy. We've got two cases all at once." Jim pulled a legal pad off the top of the file cabinet and sat down in his desk chair. His hands were shaking. He'd only written a few sentences when remorse couldn't be pushed down any longer. "I'm sorry guys. I'm glad you came in, Tony. Hank, thanks for calling him. Do you mind writing the report? Letting me dictate?"

"You know I don't, Boss." Hank Mills took the pen and pad from him. "Shoot!"

When both incidents were thoroughly documented, Jim thanked them again, agreed to take the next day off, and drove home.

There was a note stuck in the door, no envelope just a note. "Sorry if I shouldn't have called your Deputy. It just seemed like the right thing at the time. If I was wrong, forgive me?" And it was signed 'Helen', not Sergeant Bailey, just 'Helen.'

Again, he was baffled. He liked having Helen for a friend and no doubt she was attractive. Short, curly, dark brown hair that looked good on her, fit her petite body. But he liked long blonde hair, on tall slender women. Like Mrs. McAlpin. Patsy.

Or Polly, no matter what she looked like. And her long white curls almost put her in the category of blonds. Jim shook his head. Better not think about her.

The next morning the cell phone on the bedside table woke him up. From a great dream.

"Jim, Helen Bailey here. Sorry to bother you but I thought you'd want to know. And your office said you were off today."

Jim swallowed and tried to hide the irritation in his voice. "Yeah?"

"We got a note here at headquarters, stuck under the outside door, not through the mail."

"Yeah?"

"It just said 'Not an accident.'"

"What was it talking about?"

"I think it meant the boy's death yesterday."

"But we know that was an accident. It must be talking about some other case."

"It was in an envelope addressed to 'the lady cop.' And I don't have any other accident cases."

Jim sat up and put his legs on the floor beside his bed. "Hmm. Was it handwritten?"

"No, printed. If you have time, I thought maybe we might meet for lunch and discuss it."

Jim glanced at the clock. 11:30. But he didn't get to sleep 'til after 4 a.m. "Okay, 12:30? Where?"

"You choose."

He didn't want to go to Wendy's. Not after the last time they were there. "Captain D's?"

"See you then."

Wendy's was where she'd kissed him after telling him he needed a full-time deputy. He had two competent deputies. Just because she'd discovered the murderer that last time didn't mean he should replace the guys. It would be good to have a female for times when women needed to be dealt with. Like yesterday. Now he remembered his dream. Patsy McAlpin was kissing him, not just a friendly kiss either. Man, that was some dream. And Miss Know-it-all had interrupted before it got really good. Oh, well. No use crying over spilt milk.

Or could it have been a – what did they call it - prophetic dream? He'd heard of those. Some Christians had dreams they said were from God and told about the future. Jim glanced toward the ceiling on his way to the shower. "Anytime you want to make that happen, feel free!" But what was that discomfort. Polly didn't care about him that way. Why should he feel guilty about being attracted to somebody else?

When he reached Captain D's, Helen Bailey was already seated and motioned him over to the table. In front of her were clams, corn on the cob, and steamed broccoli. Across from her, in front of the empty seat was his favorite meal of fish, fries, and coleslaw. Yes, it was his favorite but why did she have to go and buy it for him? Like she was his mother or something.

He spoke through gritted teeth. "Thanks. Saves time. Here, I'll pay you back." He reached in his back pocket for his wallet.

She shook her head. "No, this was my idea. My treat." Then she bowed her head and began to pray over their food.

When she'd said 'Amen,' Jim picked up his fork. He couldn't believe it when he saw the cup of melted butter. He always got it for his hush puppies, but he'd never seen anyone else order it. How did she know? Ah, they ate takeout from here in his truck one day when they were waiting for someone to come out of another restaurant. And she remembered.

Before he could thank her again, she spoke. "Actually this is a guilt offering, Jim. Or a bribe for forgiveness. I've really regretted that last time when we were in Wendy's. I don't know what came over me." She lifted her shoulders and scrunched up her nose. "Can we be friends again?"

"Sure. No bribes necessary. Past forgotten."

She took a deep sigh and smiled at him. "Thank you." She leaned down to the seat beside her, pulled an envelope out of her purse, and handed it across the table.

It was lined paper, like you'd find in a classroom. In a very sloppy but readable print, the words 'To the lady cop' were on the envelope and 'It was not an accident." was scrawled across the page inside.

He looked over at her and raised his eyebrows.

"I haven't turned it in yet." She lifted her chin. "It is addressed to me!"

"What about prints?"

Her chin fell back down and took her shoulders with it. "I didn't even think about prints."

Jim laughed. "Then if there are none others, it will appear that either you or I slipped the letter in the door."

"I'm sorry. I can't believe I was so stupid."

His heart felt warmer toward her than it had for a long time, well, maybe forever. She was fallible after all. He purposefully pulled out his kindest voice. "Well, tell you what. I'll send it in from my office with another sheet of both our prints and tell them to eliminate those and find whatever else they can."

Helen's chest rose as she took a deep breath and then exhaled. Cute little thing. Jim was glad their friendship was restored. She was one of the few women he felt comfortable with, didn't have to fight intruding thoughts about her body, could just enjoy her personality.

When they finished eating and walked to their cars, Helen even gave him a quick hug – a friendship hug. He patted her shoulder and got in his car with the envelope and note.

"Promise to let you know as soon as I hear."

"Thanks," she said. "And if you need me again about the campground case, just call."

Chapter Eight

Jim and Officer Bailey had left around three o'clock, satisfied that they'd talked with everyone at the campground and gotten all the information there was to gather.

At six exactly, from the office window, Polly saw Sandy's car pull up. She hurried to the door.

Sandy grinned and stopped the car when she spotted her. She rolled down the window of her BMW. "Hey, Girlfriend!"

Polly laughed with pure joy. "Hey back! Just park over there for a minute and I'll get someone to take over the office." She pointed to a marked off parking space right beside the building. Within a few minutes June Gabbard was at the desk.

Sandy giggled when Polly unlocked the door of her Wind River Cherokee camper. "This feels like an adventure for real."

Then she apologized. "I'm sorry. I forgot somebody you know just died last night."

"It's okay. It wasn't anybody close to me so although I'm sorry he died, and sorry for his ex-wife, I don't feel any personal loss."

Polly took Sandy's bag and set it on her own bed. "I changed the sheets earlier, so you can have this room and I'll take the couch bed. It's close quarters but not as close as our dorm room at UK."

Sandy laughed. "You're right about that! So what did Jim say when you told him I was coming?"

"Uh, well ... I didn't talk to him about the change of plans so he thinks you're coming Tuesday, and he was really glad, hopes he'll see you more often."

"When will he be back out here?"

Polly shook her head. "No clue. He didn't say."

They decided on charbroiled hamburgers and homemade French fries for supper. When they were seated at the table, Sandy brought up the murder.

"So what are the clues? And which of us is Nancy Drew and which is Bess or George?"

"Well, neither one of us wants to be just a sidekick so one of us can be Nancy and the other Judy Bolton. They may never have met in the books but why not? And you can be whoever you want."

Sandy grinned. "Okay, I'll be Nancy and you be Judy."

"Agreed."

"So fill me in."

Polly reached behind her to the shelf over the table and got a notepad and pen. "Hmm, we each need one." She started to reach behind her again, but Sandy stopped her.

"Got one in my purse. Nancy Drew is always prepared." She pulled them out. "Okay, shoot. List the suspects."

"Oh dear. There are over a hundred campsites. And I guess it could have been somebody from outside. If it is, then I doubt we'll ever figure it out."

"Let's just assume the murderer is here. Which ones are most likely?"

"Tom Broughton did not have a lot of fans. He was really a good manager of the grounds and upkeep, but he had the personality of a pit bull. Well, actually I may be maligning pit bulls 'cause I really don't know what they are like. But Tom was stubborn and territorial and rude."

"So who do you think had reason to hate him enough to kill him?"

Polly drew a deep breath. "The person that comes to mind first is Bill Trent. Tom was awfully flirtatious with his wife. But that isn't enough reason to kill somebody."

"Were they having an affair?"

"Oh, I don't think so. It was just that the night before he was killed, he made it obvious that he wanted to party with her. And her husband came and played a game with some of us."

She repeated Bill's words when he lost at Victim. "'Guess I'm just a natural victim tonight.' But he seemed more sad than angry."

Sandy finished making notes and then looked up. "Who's next?"

Polly felt like a traitor. "The Rileys, but I know they wouldn't hurt ... " She stopped as she recalled the fury in Lucy Riley's voice when Tom Broughton kicked her dog. Then she recounted the incident to her friend.

Sandy's eyebrows went up a quarter inch. "Sounds like a motive to me. Been trying to get rid of him for years. Then he kicks their dog?"

"But you haven't met them. Seriously, they are older than us, and frail - no way they could have overpowered Tom Broughton. He is - was - a very muscular outdoor type. It would take a strong man to kill him without shooting or poisoning."

"Okay, you said he was killed by a blow to the forehead. Where?"

" In the kitchen of his camper, they say. So obviously he was awake when it happened."

"Oh." Sandy looked disappointed. "It really does look like it's that woman's husband doesn't it? Not much mystery to solve."

Just then Sandy's cell phone rang. She answered and then mouthed to Polly. "It's Jim. Should I tell him I'm here?"

Polly nodded, ignoring the tightening of her stomach.

Sandy laughed. "Ask her yourself. I'm here in her camper." And she handed the phone over.

"Hello?"

"I thought you said Sandy wasn't coming 'til Tuesday."

"I forgot to tell you that I called and asked her to come earlier." She could feel herself blush, hoping he didn't connect the early arrival with the murder. She didn't want to admit that they wanted to play amateur detectives.

"Hmm. Well, what I called her for was to get your phone number. I forgot to ask you for it earlier. How about me taking you two ladies to lunch tomorrow after church?"

"I'd love it! Well, let me make sure with Sandy."

She cupped her hand over the phone. "He wants to take us out to lunch tomorrow after church. Were we going to services?"

"Well... why not? But I didn't bring anything very churchy to wear. Are we going to our old church?"

Polly spoke into the phone again. "Where do you go, Jim? Where we grew up?"

"No, I go to a new non-denominational church. Want to come to mine?"

When they found out they didn't need to wear anything dressy, they asked for directions. Polly gave him her phone number, they said 'goodbye,' and she broke the connection.

Sandy was staring at her. "What is this all about?"

Polly could feel herself blushing again. "What do you mean?"

"Okay, he called me to get your number, obviously he wasn't expecting to take both of us out to lunch since he didn't know I was here. And you blushed like a teenager when you talked to him!"

"I was blushing because I didn't want the Sheriff to suspect we were playing Nancy Drew!"

"Why did he want your number?"

"He's lonely, Sandy. He misses you. He came to lunch here today and we talked a lot about the past and I asked forgiveness for the cowboy soda."

Sandy laughed. "I'd forgotten about that."

Polly saw no reason to repeat what Jim told her about his feelings for her in Junior High.

"Okay," Sandy conceded. "Now I understand."

But Polly wasn't sure she herself did.

He took them to a nice steak place for lunch after church, and Sandy ordered just the salad bar while Polly and Jim both got sirloin, medium rare. Jim ordered fries and salad with his but Polly substituted green beans for the potatoes.

As soon as they ordered, Sandy excused herself and went to the ladies' room. Polly watched her friend until the door closed behind her. Then she turned to Jim and smiled. "I liked the message this morning, Jim."

"You did?" Excitement showed in his eyes.

She laughed. "The music and stuff was unusual, I admit. It will take some getting used to."

Jim's eyes lit up. "You mean you'll come back."

She looked across the table at him. And smiled. "Yes, I'll come back. If you want me to."

"Oh, I want you," he said in a soft voice.

Sandy came back to the table and the conversation turned to people who were still living in the Frankfort area that they all had known.

Polly hoped they couldn't hear her heart pounding over the discussion.

They both waved back as Jim pulled by them and left the parking lot. Polly turned the car back toward the campground.

She could feel Sandy's eyes on her. " What did you think of that church? "

"Well, it was different. But I think I like it."

"Really? Polly, you've become almost like a stranger

in some ways recently. I always thought we were just alike."

She took her eyes off the road for just a few seconds to smile reassuringly at her friend. "We are a lot alike, Sandy. But remember, you were happily married, and I was very lonely and unhappy for a long time. You, well, you kind of look for a closer relationship with God over decades of loneliness."

"Oh."

They spent the rest of the drive back to the campground in silence.

When they turned in the entrance, Polly was horrified to see a fire engine parked in front of the office.

The fire engine was taking up the whole street in front of the office, blocking access to her camper, so Polly pulled off the road and slightly into Sam Molloy's site. She jumped out of the car and looked back at Sandy. "Do you want to come?"

Her friend shook her head. "No, thanks."

Polly hurried toward the office and saw a group of residents standing on the other side of the fire truck.

"Sam, I'm parked in your yard. Is that okay?" The older man nodded and shuffled over to her. He looked like he had aged in the last few days. She spoke more gently. "What's going on?"

He shook his head. "Somebody set a fire in Dot's camper."

"Is she okay?" What a nightmare this was turning into. And just as she'd gotten Sandy to consider her new carefree lifestyle.

"She's fine. She was in the office and saw the smoke. They got it put out in time. Only some smoke damage. And water. But she's pretty shook."

The beeping noise of the engine's back-up system sent them scurrying closer to the office door. The crowd that had gathered watched the departure in silence. But as soon as the truck disappeared around the curve, conversations broke out.

Polly turned to Sam again. "Where's Dot?"

He shook his head. "She was here a minute ago."

Polly looked down toward the lower campground where Dot's camper was situated. She could see Brenda and Dot standing by the picnic table on the patio at her spot.

She patted Sam' arm and said, "I've got a friend in my car so I'm going to move it on to my driveway.

He just nodded.

Polly started to walk back toward her car but hesitated and turned around.

"Are you okay, Sam?"

He nodded. But he didn't look sure. And she wasn't either.

Polly wished, not for the first time that day, that she hadn't asked Sandy to come early. Nothing was going the way she thought it would. Served her right for wanting to turn a human being's death into an occasion to fulfill a childhood desire to play detective.

When she and Sandy were back in her camper, she asked the question. "Do you mind if I go and see if Dot's okay?"

Sandy sighed and shook her head. "No, I think I need a nap anyway." And went back to the bedroom.

Dot and Brenda were sitting at the picnic table when Polly got there. Dot had her elbows on the table and her face in her hands. Polly shot a silent question at Brenda, who just shrugged and shook her head.

Polly gently laid her hand on Dot's shoulder. "Dot, is there anything I can do?"

Dot looked up and gave her a slight smile. "No. No, I don't think there's anything anybody can do. I guess I'll fix up something and sleep in the office 'til the camper dries out from the fire - and the smoke smell goes away." She looked over at Brenda. "Brenda helped me open all the windows - the ones that the fire department didn't break!" She said the last with sarcasm.

"Do you have insurance?" Polly kind of remembered that insurance was required of all the owners of RiversEdge.

"Oh, yes. It's not money; it's just ... " Dot shook her head. "Tom hasn't been dead over thirty-six hours and it's like everything has fallen apart."

"I'm so sorry." If she hadn't invited Sandy, Dot could stay in her camper. And Brenda and Doug didn't have room. "Could you stay in Tom's camper or would that be too painful?"

"Probably, but it's not an option. Remember it's roped off, 'til they have some team come and check it all out tomorrow."

Polly hadn't known.

Brenda broke into the conversation. "Well, tonight you are staying with me. The couch in our living room makes a bed. And you can have supper with us. Now let's go back in and see if there are any clothes we need to wash smoke smell out of."

"I'll help," Polly offered.

The three went into the camper, and it wasn't nearly as bad as Polly expected. There was a sour smoke odor but nothing like she'd feared.

"How did the fire start?"

Dot shook her head. "I saw the smoke from the office and called the fire department. They said I left a cigarette in an ashtray in the bedroom and it fell over onto the mattress."

Polly looked curiously at Brenda, and then turned back to Dot in confusion.

She nodded. "Right. I don't smoke."

Chapter Nine

The report came in on Wednesday. There was one set of prints besides Jim's and Helen's on the paper, but there were no matching ones on record.

The driver refused to give any information about the other five passengers in the back of the truck. "Just some guys, he said." Helen reported over a cola while Jim drank his black coffee.

It was three-thirty in the afternoon and they'd just attended the funeral of Jerry Andrews. Both spoke words of sorrow to his parents.

"He was a good boy." Mrs. Andrews looked back and forth between them as if trying to convince them of her son's innocence. Mr. Andrews just shook his head. "Bad crowd."

"I wonder what Jerry was really like?" Helen took a sip of her drink. She'd chosen McDonalds today. She said she was addicted to their diet cokes. "Such a waste."

"He sure wasn't particular about who he ran with,"

Jim said. "But, the McAlpin kid didn't seem too bad, come to think of it."

"Oh, yeah, you took him home, didn't you? What kind of home life."

Jim felt his face redden. "Seemed good. Mother nice and concerned. Father deserted when he was seven. Not real unusual these days."

"Mother good looking?"

Jim's face felt redder. "Not bad." He picked up his coffee and held the cup to his lips for half a minute 'til he felt comfortable again.

"You know we're going to have to interview him again. Because of the note."

"Yeah." Jim hoped he sounded nonchalant. "Want me to do it?"

"Well, it really falls under my jurisdiction." Helen paused a minute. "Want to do it together?"

Jim shrugged like it didn't matter. "Sure, why not?"

They took both cars to the McAlpin home. They'd seen Billy at the funeral and now they found him sitting in the yard alone petting a black poodle.

Jim saw that when Bill noticed them getting out of the car, he took a deep breath, as if steeling himself for their questions.

Jim broke the silence. "Hey, Billy. How're you doing?"

The kid just shook his head.

"You remember Officer Bailey?"

Billy McAlpin nodded.

"Do we have to sit on the grass, or is there some place we can talk?" Jim smiled so the boy would know it was friendly humor and not sarcasm.

He got up slowly and put the dog down. "There." He pointed to the swing and two lawn chairs on the porch.

When they were all seated, the boy on the swing and them in the chairs, Jim said, "We need to ask you a few questions, son."

Billy's eyes were blank as he looked up.

"First, we need to know who the other guys in the back of the truck were. And, did you by any chance turn around and see how Jerry fell?"

Billy shook his head again.

Jim purposefully made his voice tone as gentle as possible. "Billy, we really need a witness that saw Jerry's accident before we can close the case. Who were the others?"

The boy continued to stare at the floor of the porch. "You know I can't tell you."

Sgt. Bailey spoke for the first time. "Why, Billy? Are you afraid of them?"

The boy's first reaction was a definite head shaking of denial. Then he stopped. "I don't know. I guess."

"You think they will try to get even with you, hurt you, if you tell their names?"

"Yeah, that's it." But the dullness in his voice didn't agree with his words.

There was something not right. The McAlpin kid was showing no fear and not really any sorrow. It was like he had just withdrawn from connection with the incident. Jim looked over at Sgt. Bailey and shrugged his shoulders.

He watched Helen Bailey take a deep breath and then stand up. "Well, Sheriff Murray, looks like we'll have to book him after all."

He nodded. And she began reading his rights.

"Wait. Why are you arresting me?"

"Withholding evidence."

"Evidence? For an accident?"

"It was no accident and somebody who was in that truck bed knows. We've got to find out who, to protect his life."

For the first time, Billy's face became animated. "Can't you ask Grinch?"

"Grinch?" Helen Bailey's eyes widened.

"Grinch – the guy who was driving. They were his friends. I don't know who they were."

"If you didn't know them," Jim glared at the boy, "why did you go to Jerry Anderson's funeral?"

"Well, I knew Jerry. It was just the rest of them I didn't know."

Jim was looking at Helen trying to assess if she was going on with the arrest when another car drove up, this one into the driveway instead of parking on the street like their cars.

"What's going on here?" Patsy Alcorn resembled a mother tiger as she leaped out of the car. "All okay, Billy?"

He nodded.

Jim answered her first question. "We need to know who was in the truck bed with the boy who was killed. Your son won't tell us."

The look that passed between mother and son puzzled him. Something deep and hidden passed between them, some knowing that was incomprehensible to him, and probably to Helen, uh, Sgt. Bailey, too.

"Billy?" The woman asked her son.

"I don't know, Mom. I knew Grinch and Jerry.

That's all. They should ask Grinch."

She smiled at them, a smile that looked like it had been lying in a pickle jar for a week. "Then don't you think you officers had better leave now?"

Jim looked at Helen and she replaced the pen in her uniform pocket. She nodded at him and then at Mrs. McAlpin before speaking to Billy. "Okay, but if you find out who any of the boys were, will you be sure and call us?"

Patsy McAlpin looked at Jim and said, "I have your card, Sheriff. I promise that I will call the very moment that he finds out something about those other boys."

"Wait a minute." He pulled out a pen and wrote on the back of another card. "That's my cell number." When he handed it to Mrs. McAlpin, she smiled. And blinked her eyes. And softened her voice. "Thank you, Sheriff. I promise I'll call right away if we find out anything. And you have our number if you need us, right?"

Man, those eyes were to drown in. Jim gulped. "Yes, ma'am. I have it." He stood there without making a movement toward his squad car.

"Sheriff?" Sergeant Bailey's voice broke the silence. "Are you ready or are you staying?"

"Oh, sure." Jim turned his back on the mother and son and walked to his car. The police car left first. When they'd turned the corner, Bailey turned her right blinker on and stuck her hand out the window and motioned Jim to pull over behind her.

He watched as she locked the squad car and walked back to climb into the passenger seat beside him.

"Okay, something's fishy. First he says he can't tell

us who the kids were 'cause he's scared and then he says he doesn't know who they were. What's your take?"

"I don't know." Jim scratched his head. He hated to admit he didn't have a 'take.' Surely she wouldn't discover the truth before he did this time, not again. He hated to ask. "What's your take?"

She laughed. "I don't have one either. But something's fishy."

He nodded thoughtfully, hoping his relief didn't show.

"Okay, Sheriff. Keep me updated and I'll do the same." She opened the door and slid out of the seat. When she got to the driver's side of the police car, she turned and with a grin, saluted him before she got in and drove off.

Jim just shook his head and took off behind her.

Jim took extra care as he combed his hair. Even looked in the mirror to check it out. Mrs. McAlpin had asked him to spend some time with her son. She'd even said she hoped they'd become friends. So, he had every reason to return during his off-duty hours, didn't he?

When he pulled up in front of the house, he was relieved to see her car in the driveway.

While straightening his collar and giving one last glance in the rearview mirror at his hair, he hoped his after-shave wasn't too strong. Sometimes he got carried away with it.

He knocked on the door and Billy opened it. The

kid's eyes widened.

"Hi, Billy. Don't worry. This isn't official, just thought I'd stop by and see how you and your Mom are doing."

"Mom!" The boy turned and shouted. "It's that sheriff from the other day."

Jim heard the sultry voice float back on the air. "Tell him to come on in, honey. I'll be out in a minute."

Billy pointed to the couch and sat down in a chair on the other side of the coffee table.

"How have you been?"

The teen shrugged his shoulders. "Okay."

"Hadn't heard from you so I guess you haven't found out who those other four kids were?"

Billy shook his head.

They sat in silence. Jim couldn't think of a single thing to say. He was glad the TV was on. The boy stared at it, apparently fascinated.

Finally, Mrs. McAlpin walked into the room. Dear God in heaven! She was in a negligee set. Not anything you could see through but boy, could you imagine!

"I'm sorry, Sheriff, that I'm not dressed. Well," she smiled shyly, "I mean in regular clothes. I was just getting out of the bath when you rang the bell."

He stood up. His mother taught him that gentlemen always stand up when ladies come into the room. He only wished he'd done it right away but it took a few seconds of staring before he remembered.

She took the TV control out of her son's hand. He looked up at her with narrowed eyes that returned to their normal size when she looked back at him. "We'll turn off the TV now and visit with our guest."

She moved to the couch, sat down, and patted the

cushion beside her where Jim had been seated. "Sit down, Sheriff, and make yourself comfortable. What brings you our way?"

"Um, you said, uh." He didn't want to say she'd asked him to befriend her son, not with the boy sitting there. Why hadn't he called first? "I just wanted to make sure you two were all right. That there hasn't been any unpleasantness since the, um, incident, the accident."

She reached out and put her hand on his which was lying on his knee. "Aren't you the sweetest thing! No, Sheriff, no unpleasantness at all." She patted his hand and let hers linger a moment before she withdrew it.

His head was swimming, just a little, from her touch. Well, maybe it was from her perfume too. Heavy. If his after-shave was too strong, it didn't matter. Her perfume drove out every other scent around it.

He looked over at the teen who was watching his Mom with what appeared to be great interest. "Billy tells me he hasn't found out anything about the other kids in the truck."

"No, he hasn't." She leaned back and put her feet up on the coffee table. "So, tell us, Sheriff, any interesting crimes going on in the county. "

"No, Ma'am. Just the usual speeding tickets and drunk driving, couple of non-coms. Uh, non-compliances with licenses - fishing, hunting. Usually the game guys take care of that but they've asked me to help 'cause one of their guys has been off sick." He didn't mention the murder at the campground. Why? Because Polly was there and thinking about it made him feel guilty that he was here. Why, for heaven's sake? Polly only saw him as a younger brother.

She patted his arm this time. "I'm sure you are a great help to all the other law enforcement agencies. We are very lucky to have you in our county."

Then before he could think of anything else to say, Mrs. McAlpin continued. "That was a very pretty police officer with you when you came last time. Are you together often?"

"Naa, just when the territory overlaps. Or I need a female to talk to female suspects or something."

She cocked her head and said in a teasing sort of voice, "Come now, Sheriff. As pretty as she is and as handsome as you are, surely there is more to your relationship than work?"

He tried to keep the irritation out of his voice. "No, just work."

He turned to Billy, who was still staring at his mother. "Have you had supper yet? I thought maybe we could go grab a hamburger or something."

Billy looked at him with surprise. "Uh, no, Sir. I, uh. I guess. Is that okay, Mom?"

Patsy McAlpin stared into her son's eyes. "Well of course, but Sheriff, we'd love to have you stay here and have supper with both of us. That way, I get to know you better too." When she'd finished speaking, she turned back to him and smiled. "Okay?"

He grinned. "Okay. Thanks, Patsy, I'd love it."

"Great." She stood up. "Billy would you start the grill? I'll change into... something less comfortable?" She laughed and left the room.

Jim followed the teen out the sliding glass doors into the back yard. It was spacious with a wooden privacy fence all around and a flower garden in one corner. A round glass top table sat at one end of the con-crete patio, and a built-in old-fashioned brick grill was on the other end. Billy grabbed a bag of charcoal and a can of lighter fluid from a cabinet that stood against the house to one side of the glass doors.

Just as the fire was leaping several feet above the grill, Mrs. McAlpin – Patsy – joined them. This time she was in navy blue shorts and a white lowcut sleeve-less top. "I hope hamburgers are still okay? That's what we were having anyway?"

"Sure, even better on the grill." Jim relaxed. This felt good. Made him wish he was married. A pretty woman, a kid, nice house, yard, garden. Normal life. Maybe...

Chapter Ten

W hen Sandy woke up from her nap, Polly filled her in on the fire and they resumed the roles of Nancy Drew and Judy Bolton. It didn't quite feel the same for Polly; she realized that the fun had been driven out of the adventure by concern for Dot and something uncomfortable she was feeling about Sam Molloy.

That night she and Sandy watched a DVD of "The Trouble With Angels," a Haley Mills film they had identified with when they were in high school. The two friends in the movie were always getting into trouble in the convent school they attended, just as Polly and Sandy had sometimes gotten into trouble at church camp. For smoking, for skipping out on things they were supposed to attend, for going places they shouldn't.

"But at least neither of us ended up a religious fanatic," Sandy said, when Haley Mills' character announced to her friend that she was becoming a nun.

Polly nodded but felt uncomfortable for the first

time since the movie started.

"That role was taken by our little brother, right?"

Feeling like a traitor, Polly answered, "Right."

A knock on the camper door around eleven on Thursday sent Sandy running back to the bedroom in her nightgown. Polly. who was already dressed, opened to find Jim standing on the patio. Looking great.

"Hi, come in."

He did and pulled the door behind him.

"It's just Jim," Polly yelled back toward the bedroom.

"I'm almost dressed. Be right out."

Polly motioned to the table and chairs by the extension window. "Take a seat. We were just having coffee. Want some?"

He shook his head. "No thanks. Gave it up."

"Really? Is that some religious thing or something?"

Jim laughed with that twinkle in his eye that had become like an electric charge aimed at her stomach. "No, just decided I didn't like being addicted."

Sandy came in, gave him a hug, and sat in the chair beside him. "What are you doing out here?"

"Two things. Came with the forensics team to complete the examination of Tom Broughton's camper. They were going to do it yesterday but got tied up on something else. And to check out the report of the fire in his ex-wife's place."

Polly filled Sandy's coffee cup and sat down at the third chair. "Did you find out that Dot doesn't smoke, and the fire began with a cigarette?"

He nodded, all the twinkle replaced by seriousness. "You girls have any ideas?"

"What do you mean?" Polly refused to look at Sandy.

"Oh, come on. I'm not too old to remember how you two liked to play detective. I know why Sandy came early."

Sandy blushed too and they both laughed.

"Caught in the act." Polly bowed her head in acquiescence. "But no, we don't have anything except a suspicion that Bill Trent could have done it out of jealousy."

Jim didn't comment.

Polly had hoped he would tell them something of interest by agreeing or disagreeing.

"And we can't see any motive for him to set fire to Dot's place." Polly hated admitting defeat.

Jim nodded. "She used to be married to Broughton. Could there be some financial motive for somebody to get rid of both of them?"

"But the fire was in the daytime while Dot was in the office! They knew she wouldn't be hurt!" Polly protested.

"Would that, coming so fast on the death of her ex make her want to leave the campground? Can you explain to me how the ownership works?"

"I could sort of, but Brenda Croft could do a much better job. Want me to call her? Oh, I forgot. Our friendship is supposed to be under cover."

Jim dismissed his original request with a shake of his head. "It would look really strange if they found out Sandy's my sister. So we'll just act normal and tell the truth if asked. Okay?" He smiled at Polly. "Go ahead and ask your friend to come over. Or would you rather I went there?"

"No!" Polly hoped she didn't sound too eager to have every minute possible in his company. Her hands shook slightly as she punched in Brenda's number on the cell phone.

Her neighbor arrived within five minutes and Polly and Sandy moved to the couch to allow them privacy for their conversation. Polly tried to think of something to talk about, but her mind was filled with the presence of Jim Murray. Sandy finally asked if she had read a recent fiction best seller and Polly had, so they discussed it for the rest of the time Brenda and Jim discussed campground fiscal policy and whatever else he asked her.

When the two got up from the table, he said, "I'm going to tell Ms. Broughton she can go in her ex-husband's camper now. She was at the office last I saw. Think she's still there?"

Brenda nodded. "She's staying with me so if she isn't there come to number sixteen."

It was only about thirty minutes later when another knock sounded on the door of Polly's camper. This time the open door revealed Dot Broughton.

Polly invited her in.

"I hate to bother you, but I wondered if you and Brenda might come with me to Jim's camper. Your friend could come too if she wants." Dot nodded to Sandy who was watching TV.

"No thank you. But you go on, Polly. I'm fine."

When they got to the manager's camper, Brenda was sitting at the picnic table waiting. She stood up and followed them inside. Dot shivered. And shook her head.

"The last time I was here ... " She put her hand to her throat.

Polly immediately hugged her. "Try not to think about it, Dot. Try to remember some good times."

Tears filled the manager's ex-wife's eyes. "That's almost worse. I had such hopes. Thought at last I'd found The One! You know?"

Polly didn't know but saw Brenda nodding. The One? She'd never experienced "The One." Could it be that was what she was beginning to feel ... Ridiculous. Not at sixty-two!

Dot straightened up. "I'm okay. Now if you all will help me sort out some papers, I'd really appreciate it. I have to find some financial information and a will, if there is one."

Dot brought drawers and boxes from the hallway closet, bedroom shelves, and living room cabinets. Soon they were seated at the table with a huge pile in the middle.

"How do you want to sort them?" Polly was surprised that the efficient Dot hadn't already told them.

Dot took a deep breath. "Okay, let's make three piles - lists and personal notes and correspondence, bills and bank statements - anything financial, and , well, I guess just "other."

"Do you want to go through them first and we'll make the piles or should we all just start in?" Brenda asked.

"Oh, all just start in, if you don't mind."

They assured her they didn't mind and started in.

It seemed to Polly that Tom Broughton was a great list maker. There were penciled sheets of paper with check marks beside them in almost everything she picked up. Most were just lists of chores or equipment.

The checkbook showed unexpected and unexplained deposits of cash from $500 to $2,000. And the current balance was over thirty thousand dollars.

"When we were married, he never had this kind of money," Dot said. "And that hasn't been very long ago."

"What's this?" Brenda's voice had a strident tone Polly had never heard before.

She handed it to Dot, who read aloud.

"Colonel Idiot -Sat - 2

Dr. Trent - Sat - 1

Sal - Wed - 1/2"

She shook her head. "What in the world could that be?"

Judy Bolton took over. "Could it be a list of blackmail victims?" Polly asked hesitantly.

Dot looked horrified. "Surely ... " She stopped and said nothing else.

"I think we should turn this list over to the sheriff," Polly said firmly.

"I agree," said Brenda, looking at Dot for final approval.

She nodded slowly.

Brenda said, "Looks to me like he went into the blackmailing business." Polly had to agree with her.

They'd almost completed dispersing the papers into the three piles when Polly came across a paper from one of the bedroom drawers and gasped involuntarily.

The others stopped what they were doing and looked at her. She didn't say anything but turned the paper around and handed it to them.

"No more messin' with my wife or it's all cut off. Get it?"

"I won't!" Polly glared up at Jim Murray.

"Don't be stupid, Polly. It could be dangerous here." He glared back. "You don't need to stay. You could go with Sandy or both of you come to my place."

Sandy suddenly smiled. "Of course we could. I don't mean go to Jim's, but we could go to Louisville and you could stay with me 'til all this is solved. We'd have so much fun." She looked pleadingly at Polly. "And we'd be safe."

"No." Polly turned to look at her friend. "If you want to go, that's fine. I won't get mad or anything. But I'm staying right here. This is my home!"

Sandy sighed. "Well, it's certainly not where I'd want to stay."

Polly forced herself to un-grit her teeth. "Then you go on home. It won't hurt my feelings. All this isn't what I'd planned for you to experience when I invited you."

"No!" Jim turned to his sister. "I don't want her left alone. I mean, she really shouldn't stay here by herself. She'll be safer if someone is with her."

"Hey, little brother, I'm a big girl now and can take care of myself." Polly could have bitten her tongue the minute the words came out of her mouth. The hurt in Jim's eyes when she called him 'little brother' was obvious. But she couldn't take them back now. So she just put her face in her hands and shook her head. And, besides, he deserved it for calling her stupid!

The next thing she knew, a warm strong hand was squeezing her shoulder.

"I'm sorry, Polly. I shouldn't have said it was stupid to decide to stay here. Forgive me. I'm just worried about you. About both of you." When she didn't respond, he sighed and took his hand away.

She heard the scraping sound of a chair being pulled back and looked up as Jim lowered himself into the chair beside her.

"Okay, ladies, I'm going to tell you something." He looked first at Sandy and then at Polly.

"Bill Trent knows that Polly and Brenda Croft were with Dot in the camper when she found the documents. He swears he didn't write the threatening note and since it was printed, we can't prove it one way or another. But the "Doctor Trent" part ... "

Polly nodded. "Yes, I've wondered about that. What did it mean?"

"Bill Trent has been known in the past to deal in drugs, mainly pills. Not a user. So I think the "Doctor Trent" stands for 'the Trent who hands out pills'. He denied knowing anything about it. Of course."

"What about "Colonel Idiot?" Polly was afraid she knew the answer to that one.

Jim said, "We're checking that out. Not sure. Clayton Wylie is a Lt. Colonel retired from the US Army."

"And Sal?"

"No clue. But comparing that list with some bank deposits over the past few months it appears that the numbers could refer to thousands of dollars. Two thousand, one thousand, and the half could mean five hundred dollars."

"So what you're saying is that you suspect Bill Trent. He was being blackmailed by Tom and killed him?"

"Either being blackmailed or getting a part of the take for letting the action take place here at the campground."

Polly's stomach suddenly sent out waves of nausea. Her haven? Her refuge, a drug dealership?

Jim gently put his hand over hers there on the table. "You see why I want you to get out for a while?"

Polly nodded slowly. "I see. But I can't do it."

He didn't respond except to nod his head in resignation.

Chapter Eleven

J im went back to the McAlpin's home on Friday
night, this time at Patsy's request. When he rang
the bell this time, she answered. She was in
shorts and another low-cut top, one that showed exactly where her bathing suit began. Her eyes sparkled
when she saw him, and she reached out with both
hands to draw him into the house.

She turned and opened her mouth as if she was
going to call her son but then stopped and turned
back to him. "Bill's in his room. Getting ready to go to
a football game. I had forgotten when I invited you. Do
you mind it being just us tonight?"

Jim swallowed. "No, Ma'am. Not if you don't." He
needed this distraction from Polly who still thought of
him as 'little brother." There off and on for a couple of
days, he had hoped but...

She giggled. And tucked her arm around his as
they walked into the living room.

The TV was showing a rerun of CSI. CSI somewhere, Miami it looked like. Patsy picked up the con-

trol and turned it off. "Ah, peace! Bill has been watching CSI and Law and Order constantly. I think he started it with that unfortunate boy who was killed." She shook her head. "Poor thing. Jerry, I think. Is that right?"

"Yes, Ma'am."

"Sheriff, you don't have to call me Ma'am. I'm just Patsy. Okay?" She quirked her head to an angle and grinned at him. "Okay?"

He smiled and relaxed. "Okay."

The honking of a horn sounded outside and through the window Jim saw an old Chevy. It seemed to be full already. Of boys.

"Billy! Your ride's here."

A door opened about half way down the hall and Bill came out, throwing a jacket over his shoulder as he turned to shut it.

When he reached the front door, his mother said, in a soft voice. "Don't forget your backpack, son."

With a face of stone, Bill opened the door to the closet there to the right as you walked in the house and pulled out a backpack with UK emblems on it. With a sigh, he slung it over his shoulder.

They stood in silence watching him down the walkway to join his friends. When the car had pulled away, Billy inside it, Patsy shook her head and turned to Jim. "It's hard being a single Mom."

She looked so scared and helpless, Jim almost was tempted to propose right then and there, to say "I'll help you raise him." But instead he asked, "Are those the same boys he was with the night of the... uh... accident?"

"No, I don't think so. I told him not to go with that

bunch anymore."

Jim remained quiet but thought that if a kid of his had been with a wild bunch, he'd make sure who they were going out with now.

She grinned at him. "We're all alone now."

He wasn't sure what that meant but said, "Yes, we are." What did she expect him to do?

"I've got steaks," she said as she walked toward the kitchen. "Want to get the grill going?"

"Sure." Jim went through the sliding glass doors and repeated what he saw Billy do the other time he ate here.

Helen brought the steaks out on a large tray, big steaks, T-bones. Wow. She must have plenty of money. Or was she trying to impress him?

She grinned up at him. "How do you like yours cooked?"

He grinned back. "Medium rare. How about you?"

"The same. I've got baked potatoes in the oven and they're done now. I'll throw the salad together if you want to cook the steaks."

"Sure." He watched as she put the tray on the table and walked back into the house.

Then she turned. "What kind of dressing? I've got Bleu Cheese and Ranch and French. And I can make Thousand Island if you'd rather."

"Bleu Cheese is my favorite."

She smiled again and nodded.

The meal was wonderful, made more so by the candles gleaming on the silver holders and the beauty who sat across from him. By some miracle he cooked the steaks to perfection, and Patsy's complementary words and adoring eyes completed the setting of absolute contentment.

After dinner, they did the dishes together while romantic music flowed from the boom box on the kitchen counter.

Patsy put the last plate away and turned to him, her eyes seeking his, and her chest rising and falling with what appeared to be passion. For him.

"What shall we do now?" There was a mischievous gleam in her eyes and a suggestive tone in her voice.

He swallowed hard, but no words came to his mind. She stepped closer and reached up to put her arms around his neck. He leaned down to the lips that were offered to him.

And stopped. The signal went off on his phone.

"Murray here." He hoped he didn't sound as irritated as he felt.

"Morales here." His deputy sounded serious. "Sorry to bother you, boss. But we've got trouble."

Jim sighed. "Let's have it."

"You told us to keep an eye on that place on 127? Well we did, really thought nothing would happen 'til after the game, but a bunch of the kids skipped and went straight to party."

"You caught 'em?"

"Yep, I guess they weren't expecting us 'til after the game either."

"Where are you now?"

"Still here. Hank and I got 'em. There's about twelve. Should we call the city police for back up?"

Jim looked at Patsy and sighed. "Do that and I'll be right there."

"Right boss."

He broke the connection and shrugged his shoulders. "Sorry, got a problem. I have to go. I sure hate to leave." He wondered if God had just saved him from something.

Her eyes looked as sorrowful as he felt.

"What's happened?"

He shook his head. He wasn't so far gone to ignore professional confidence. "Tell you later." He gave her a quick hug.

One of these days maybe...

He turned on the lights and siren and sped out toward the site. He hadn't gone far when he spotted more blue lights behind. Three city police cars were joining him.

They were at the deserted farm within seven minutes of the call. As he turned in, his heart sank. One of the cars sitting empty was the '04 red Toyota Camry that he'd watched Billy enter less than two hours ago.

Mills and Morales were standing on either side of a group of boys seated on the ground, most looking sullen and with narrowed eyes. Jim cast his eyes over the crowd and saw what he was looking for. Billy McAlpin was there. But he had his head down on his knees, buried in his arms.

Hank was holding the very backpack that Jim had watched the kid take with him from the hall closet at his home.

Jim walked over to Hank as the city police exited their cars and surrounded the seated boys. He pointed to the backpack with a questioning look.

"Mostly empty" was the deputy's response. "But definitely the source. There are still a few percs and gabbys in there. But the weed is all gone except for a little evidence in the bottom."

Jim's heart sank. He remembered Patsy's words to her son, the soft voice saying. "Don't forget your backpack, son."

Surely not.

But he watched with a heavy heart as Helen Bailey and the other officers marched the boys to the official cars – three to each city car and three to his deputy's car. There would be two officers to each three kids. He would stay there with the two cars belonging to the boys and wait for the tow truck.

Helen looked back at him as she escorted Billy McAlpin into the car she would drive back to town. It was a look of sorrow.

He was glad when they drove away. He didn't need her pity. It wasn't long until the tow truck came to take away the first car and they were back within twenty minutes for the second.

Jim decided to go back to the Sheriff's office. Surely Mills or Morales would come to report what had been discovered. There were plenty of experts; he wouldn't be needed at police headquarters.

He was sitting there, halfway through reading the newspaper, when the phone rang. It was Helen.

"Billy McAlpin wants to talk to you, Jim. He says he won't talk to anybody else."

Jim nodded even though he knew Helen couldn't see him. "Be right there." Then he realized she didn't have to be the one to call. "Thanks, Helen."

When he walked in Police Headquarters, there were a lot of parents standing around. But no sign of Patsy McAlpin. He was glad; he didn't want to face her. Helen stuck her head out of one of the interview rooms and motioned him to join her.

She and Billy were the only ones in the room. The boy had tears streaming down his face. He stood up when Jim walked in. And looked him straight in the eye.

"I'm sorry, Sir. It was me. I furnished the drugs. It was all me."

Jim resisted the urge to go hug the boy. The regret on his face was not faked. And the truth of the matter got more vivid in Jim's mind. He motioned the boy to sit back down. And then he and Helen sat across the table from him.

"Where'd you get the drugs, son?"

Billy looked at the table. "I'd rather not say."

"Son. Look at me." The boy slowly lifted his head. "Remember I was there when you were told not to forget your backpack." The boy's head dropped again but he quickly raised it and looked Jim directly in the eye.

He nodded. "Yes, Sir. You were." Tears filled the boy's eyes again. "I'm sorry." Then he could hold it no longer and the sobs started. "It's all my fault. Jerry's dead and it's all my fault about everything." Jim could barely understand him through the choking. "Jerry was my only friend. My first friend ever. He made me want to be one of the good guys. I didn't know what would happen or I'd never have let him come with me to be with them." He waved his hand as though to indicate the group outside the room. "I wouldn't have let him be killed."

"Where did you get the drugs, son?" Jim repeated.

Billy wiped his tears with his hand and grabbed a tissue from the table. After he blew his nose, he said. "You know."

Unfortunately, Jim did know. "Your Mom?"

The boy nodded, misery filling every feature.

Helen spoke for the first time. "Billy, was it you who sent me the note?"

Jim expected the boy to ask "What note." But he only nodded.

After a long sigh, he spoke again. "I got to sit in the front since I furnished the stuff. And I heard Grinch yell back to one of the others, "Ditch the spy!" He did that as soon as he saw that he was blocked in on both sides. Some of the other guys threw Jerry out..." His voice broke again and the sobbing started. "I'm sorry. I'm so sorry."

Helen excused herself then and said, "I'll be back in a minute."

Jim sat there feeling helpless as the teen cried again and used more tissues.

"Billy, I saw some parents out there. Did they call your mother?"

He nodded. "She's probably gone."

"Gone?"

"Yeah. She always told me if I got caught, she'd leave. She said they'd be easy on me but not her, cause she's grown up."

"But..." Jim's mind couldn't take it in. "But what would you do, where would you live?"

The boy shrugged his shoulders. "She said they

might put me in a group home or something for kids that get in trouble. Or in foster care."

The passion that had filled Jim's heart for Billy's mother changed tone. From romantic to anger. And a protectiveness he'd never experienced overflowed from somewhere toward the kid.

Just then the door opened and Helen rejoined them. She looked at Jim with a pained expression. But she spoke to the boy.

"Bill, we called your Mom, but she's never shown up. Now she's not answering the home phone. Do you have a cell phone number for her?"

The kid shook his head. "It won't work now."

Helen looked puzzled. "What do you mean?"

The boy looked up at Jim.

"I think Ms. McAlpin has probably flown the coop, as they say. Probably left that phone. And she's probably in another car?" The last was a question addressed to Billy, who nodded.

Sheriff Jim Murray decided Helen Bailey was worth a million dollars. She never mentioned that Jim was obviously having a date with the drug dealer the night that the truth all came out. He never had to tell her how close Patsy had come to making him a 'patsy'.

But he couldn't make himself think of Helen as anything but a friend. His heart was definitely regressing to his teenage years. No matter how impossible any fulfillment looked...

Chapter Twelve

S andy didn't leave, and Friday night Polly talked her into going to the shelter around six. The weekly dance at the pavilion was cancelled because of the death and funeral. For some reason Polly couldn't put her finger on, she didn't feel comfortable taking the Victim game. Maybe because the last time they'd played it, Bill Trent was the fourth.

Brenda and Dot joined them and they all opted to play hearts. The Bridge Bunch were back in their regular table spot. Everything seemed normal. To Polly's great relief, Sandy and Brenda were soon talking fiction and appeared to have a lot of favorite novels in common.

Dot broke up the game earlier than usual, saying she had a lot to do. "Visitation for Tom is going to be here tomorrow night down at the pavilion and then the funeral will be Sunday afternoon. His brother and mother are coming and maybe some cousins or something; he never had a child by any of his wives. The funeral home will bring Tom's body out tomorrow night

and take him back after visitation and bring him back
out for the funeral."

"Where will he be buried?" Polly was curious. Surely burial would not be on the campground property
also!

"At a family plot up in Eastern Kentucky. They'll
follow the hearse up there. I'm not going."

Polly was curious to find if there was a will; they
hadn't come across one in sorting through the manager's camper. But she knew it would be rude to ask.

"Will the family be staying here?" Brenda questioned.

"No, thank God!" Dot rolled her eyes. "I only met
them once. It was immediate distrust on both sides.
They are staying in a hotel downtown. But I need to go
check on some last-minute details for the visitation.
The family is handling the funeral."

When Dot disappeared into the office, Polly turned
to Brenda. "Should we send flowers? Or something? I
don't even know a florist here anymore." She turned to
Sandy. "Been a lot of years, huh?"

Just then her cell phone rang. She smiled when
she saw Jim Murray's name where she had programmed him into her phone. "Hello?"

"What are you doing?"

"Just finished a game of hearts. What are you doing?" Her heart was pounding again.

"Nothing. Just lonesome. Wondered if you two
would like to come to my house - just for ice cream or
something."

She asked Sandy, who agreed.

"We'd love to." Polly glanced at her watch. It was
just a little after ten.

"Sandy knows how to get here."

The two friends said good-night to Brenda and went back to the camper. Polly was glad when Sandy changed clothes. She wanted to put on something more attractive herself but was afraid it would cause more speculation from her friend.

Jim lived in a nice subdivision on the same side of town as the campground. It wasn't anything like the large home his sister had in Louisville, or the house Polly sold. But it was cozy.

A white picket fence surrounded the front yard and window boxes full of impatiens adorned every window.

He greeted them on the porch, which had a swing, painted white to match the fence. He hugged his sister first and then Polly, who severely ordered herself not to faint.

When they were seated in the living room in front of a coffee table, Jim left to get the dessert. Sandy was staring at Polly.

She whispered, "Are you sure there's nothing going on between the two of you?"

Polly whispered back. "Nothing at all. What makes you say that?"

Sandy gave her a look that had always meant "Come off it." "Because the way you two act, I feel like a third wheel. Jim was always the third wheel but not anymore."

"Shh, here he comes."

He had a tray which he sat on the coffee table. It was loaded with spoons, bowls of ice cream, whipped cream, crushed pecans, Caramel syrup, and a bottle of Hershey's syrup.

"As I remember, you liked butter pecan?" He handed Sandy a bowl.

"And your favorite was raspberry swirl." He handed the second bowl to Polly. "See, when I was being so obnoxious to you two, I was also watching and making notes."

Sandy laughed. "I can't believe you remembered."

Polly didn't say anything because her stomach was doing weird things again. The phrase "madly in love with you when you were in high school" kept running through her mind, "madly in love." Finally, she squeaked out. "Thank you. So much."

Really! She'd been out of high school for forty-four years. Way past time to stop acting like a high school girl.

Jim switched on the TV. "They're playing a re-run of "Trouble with Angels." Didn't know if you girls wanted to watch it or not.

Sandy and Polly looked at each other and laughed. Polly explained.

"Thanks anyway, Jim. We already did - the other night." When she looked over at him, Jim eyes were staring into hers and she couldn't draw her own away. And she didn't want to.

"The One." The term Dot had used came to her mind. Yes. He is "The One." Oneness. Jim Murray and her. She took a deep breath just as Sandy excused herself.

"I'm going to the little girls' room. Be right back." And Sandy disappeared into the hallway.

What now? Polly still didn't tear her eyes away from Jim. He didn't withdraw from the connection either but got up and walked toward her. He took her hand and lifted it to his lips.

A thrill like she'd never known shot through her body as he kissed her fingers.

"We'll talk later." He finally turned his eyes away, first to her hand and then to her hair. He let go of her hand and touched her hair. And returned to his recliner.

He smiled and said gently, "Eat your ice cream before it melts."

She and Sandy left around eleven-thirty. Polly was glad that Sandy drove because she still felt drunk. She knew they had discussed old friends and things they'd done when they were young, but it was all a blur to Polly. She was still intoxicated with the look, the kiss on the fingers, the touch of his hand on her hair.

Sandy stayed at the camper, so Polly went by herself to the visitation at four Saturday afternoon. She could have kicked herself for forgetting about sending flowers. Her mind was still not working at peak form. She decided to wait 'til the funeral was over and Tom's family left, and then she'd do something special for Dot. Maybe take her to dinner in Lexington or something.

She looked for a casket, but then spotted a small table draped with a velvet maroon cloth with a box sitting on top. And realized Tom Broughton had been cremated. She thought they used urns. But, sure enough, it was a box.

Polly assumed that the strangers greeting campground residents and other strangers were Tom's family. But she wasn't there because of them. She looked around and saw Dot talking to Sam Molloy, and joined them.

Dot's face flooded with gratitude. Polly smiled at Sam; his straight white hair was hanging down over his ears and, as usual, she wanted to take him to a barber. He still looked frazzled, and she remembered there was something she was uncomfortable with, something to do with Sam. But what?

She looked around. "Where are the Rileys and Colonel Wylie?"

Sam looked uncomfortable. "Uh, mm, I don't think they will be coming."

Dot emitted a very short sound that sounded like it might have been a laugh.

"Can you blame 'em? Tom constantly did things on purpose to irritate them."

"No, I guess not. But honestly, I'm not here because of Tom. I'm here because of you, Dot."

"I know. And I appreciate it."

Sam cleared his throat. "And I, Ma'am."

Dot smiled at him, just as Brenda and Doug Croft joined them.

"I really ought to take you over and introduce you to Tom's family," Dot said.

"That's okay," Brenda responded. "We just came to tell you how sorry we are. That you had to go through this." Her husband smiled and nodded.

"Dot, if you don't mind, I should get back to my friend. But I want us to get together soon."

"That's fine. I'm okay, really. I mean we'd been divorced half a year. My only real concern now is if the new manager will let me keep my job as assistant." Dot looked from one face to another.

It was Doug Croft who finally answered. "I imagine, Ms. Broughton, that will be one of the interview points that are discussed with applicants."

Dot smiled at him. Polly said good-bye to them all and gave Dot a hug and started back to her camper.

"Ms. Nichols." Sam's raspy voice halted her and she waited for him. The slight hill to the upper campground was no big deal to Polly but obviously a strain for the older man.

"Sam, please call me Polly. I call you Sam. Please."

He nodded. "Okay, Ms. Polly." She didn't argue with him about the Ms.

He pulled out a handkerchief and wiped his forehead. "You know, I found myself wanting to take that box and pour the ashes out on the ground and stomp on them."

Polly's eyes flew open and no words came to her mind.

"If anybody ever deserved what he got, it was that awful man." Polly remembered the day when Tom had kicked the Riley's dog and later made fun of the Colonel's bridge skills.

She said gently, "He wasn't very nice to your friends, was he?"

He shook his head. "No, not at all. He should have been relieved of his position long ago."

They reached the top of the hill and Sam turned toward his own camper which was right past Colonel Wylie's.

Sam Molloy. What was it about Sam Molloy that had been bothering her?

She let her mind play back over the conversations she'd had with him.

Sunday, when they got back from church and lunch with Jim, the fire truck, Sam saying " Somebody set a fire in Dot's camper."

How did he know somebody set a fire? At that time, the firemen thought it was an accident.

Polly closed the door to the camper.

She called out, not too loud, in case Sandy was asleep, "Nancy Drew, are you awake?" Sandy came out from the bedroom.

"Judy Bolton, is that you? What's up?"

Polly grinned at her. "Sit down and let's have some coffee."

She told her friend how violently Sam Molloy had reacted to the box of ashes at the visitation, and what she'd remembered about what he said the day of the fire.

"That little old man? I can't see him overpowering Tom Broughton, not from your description." Sandy voice was full of skepticism.

"Me neither. But the anger was there, no, it was fury. And he knew somebody had set that fire."

"Okay," Sandy said as she got her purse from the end table and pulled out her notepad and pen. "Let's look at all the suspects again ... Bill Trent, our favorite suspect, the scumbag."

Polly snickered. And breathed a sigh of relief. This felt like life almost back to normal.

Sandy went on with the list.

"Jill Trent. Hey, where has she been? I've only seen her once since I've been here and then it was just that Brenda pointed her out when she was walking out of the office."

"Probably in mourning for her lover. Not much taste in men, that girl. Neither her husband or her lover are, were, nice people. Frankly, she's not very nice either." Polly told Sandy about Jill's taunting them about playing a childish game.

"But would she have had a motive to kill Broughton?"

"I don't know unless he dumped her for somebody else. But I sure didn't see any sign of that the night before he died."

"Okay, next. The Rileys. They seem like such a nice, very genteel, couple. I see why you were so adamant about it not being them." Sandy hesitated with the pencil held above their names.

"Right. And why would they have set a fire in Dot's kitchen? Well, for that matter why would anybody? It doesn't make sense. Unless Jim hit on something when he said there could be a financial motive." Jim. Just saying his name out loud was enough to completely distract her.

"Polly?" Sandy was staring across the table at her. "Earth to Polly. Did you think of something?"

"Think of something?" Polly's mind raced to think of something. "Colonel Wylie. Surely he's on our list."

"Yes, what did you think of?"

"Umm, just thinking about his name being on that list we think could have been about blackmail, and he might have had a motive to set Dot's camper on fire to keep her from finding out anything when she did get access to Tom's place." Okay, pretty lame but it was something.

"But why wouldn't he have set Tom's place on fire?" Sandy looked at her curiously.

"Right." Dead end to that.

Just then Sandy's cell phone rang, and she opened it.

"Hi, little Brother!"

Polly's heart skipped a beat this time.

Sandy held the phone next to her chest. "He wants to know if he can take us out for supper."

"Up to you," Polly managed to say.

"Sure, why not?" Sandy spoke into the phone. "What time and where?"

When she hit disconnect she looked at Polly. "You are meeting him at Frisch's in forty-five minutes."

"Frisch's?"

"He said to remind you that it's on the other side of town now."

Polly nodded. "But you said 'you,' not 'we.' What do you mean?"

Sandy stood up and put her hands on her hips. "I mean that I am going to develop a headache, and you and Jim are going to have dinner alone and let's see what happens."

Polly shocked herself by bursting into tears. She could tell by Sandy's expression that she'd shocked her friend too.

"Hey, what's this about?" She walked over and pulled Polly's head to her shoulder and wrapped her arms around her.

Polly could barely get the words out. "Scared. Never felt like this. Ever. Walter hasn't even crossed my mind this week. I ache inside when I think of Jim. Jim! I never thought of him that way. Not ever. Or anybody else either."

"Well guess what? You are now. And he's thinking of you that way too. Now go wash your face, and get your makeup on, and get going!"

Chapter Thirteen

Jim was just walking out the door of his house when his cell phone rang.

"Okay, you owe me!" It was Sandy.

"What do you mean?"

"Polly just left to meet you at Frisch's."

"You aren't coming?"

"No, I very conveniently developed a headache. But listen, little brother, you better not break her heart."

He said, "It would be more likely that she breaks mine."

There was a moment of silence. Then his sister answered.

"That's how I thought you felt. But no, Jim, this is definitely mutual." She laughed. "I can almost feel the heat every time you two are in the same room."

"But it's not..."

"I know. It's not just physical attraction. I think it's the real thing. And I hope so. Okay, have fun! Love you." And she hung up.

Jim's heart was beating hard in his chest as he

started the car. Mutual? Polly love him? He thought about the past couple of months - first that Stephanie and then Patsy. How stupid was he? He prayed out loud "Lord, what is wrong with me that I fall for women like that? And yet I'm in love with one of the kindest, most beautiful woman in the world. She wouldn't love me if she knew about all the lust I've given in to."

Then it dawned on him. He'd never actually done anything with either of the women. Yes, it was lust, but not fulfilled. "Thank you, Lord. You stopped actual physical sin from happening both times. Looking back, I can see that now."

He was getting close to Frisch's and he prayed again. "Lord, please keep my love for Polly pure."

Suddenly it was though he was surrounded by warmth and light. He pulled off the road into a shopping center parking lot. And he was silently bathed in the love of God that enveloped him, that understanding, unconditional love greater than he had ever experienced. As the overwhelming Presence lessened, slowly the revelation came to him. He'd felt physical lust after women of no spiritual substance because he spent decades trying to ignore the love he had for Polly. The love that hadn't ever really stopped.

Then a saying he had seen on a church sign came to his mind "If God seems far away, guess who moved?" And he saw it even more clearly. Because he moved away from the painful emotion of real love unrequited, he was vulnerable to women with wrong motives, including his ex-wife.

Helen came to mind. She was pretty and nice, and he had not been attracted to her at all, even though she obviously cared about him. He felt an ache for her.

"Lord, give her somebody that will love her the way she deserves."

Then he looked at his watch. Time had stood still while he was so enveloped in the Lord's Presence. Ah, still on time; he started the car. And looked toward heaven. "Jesus is Lord!"

Polly pulled in the parking lot of the favorite restaurant of her youth. The food tasted the same - she'd come here for lunch the day she checked out the campground and loved it. Now it was in a different location from the teen years. But right now the thought of food, any food, made her nauseated.

She got out of the car and saw Jim waiting for her near the door. He smiled and then looked at the passenger side and gave her a questioning look?

"Where's big sister?" He opened the door for her to walk inside. And the second door.

Polly swallowed to moisten her throat which had gone completely dry.

"Uh, she said she was developing a headache." There, that wasn't a lie. That was what Sandy had said.

"Good for her!" Jim's voice was jubilant. "Tell her I owe her."

Polly didn't say anything and she couldn't look at him. She was sixty-two years old, for heaven's sake, acting like an adolescent.

The hostess led them to the far room surrounded by windows, to a table in the corner. She took their drink order, two waters, and left menus with them.

"What do you want? Still Big Boy and fries?" Jim's voice sounded gentle, but she couldn't make herself look at him.

"No, I've changed over the years. I want a fish sandwich and salad." She kept studying the menu.

When the waitress came back, Jim gave their order. After she left, he spoke softly.

"Polly, please look at me."

She did. And it happened again. The One. Oneness, the connection. There wasn't really a need for words. She could never verbalize what she felt pouring forth from her heart.

Jim reached across the table and took her hand without breaking the connection. Polly remembered hearing that eyes were the windows of the soul. She'd never understood that until now, 'til the other night at his house.

They sat for a long time, holding hands and pouring their hearts out in the silence. She had questions, but she didn't even know how to ask them. It would be foolish when the answers were already there, somewhere. In the mind of God?

The waitress brought their plates and they turned their eyes to her and dropped hands.

"Thank you," Jim said to the woman.

Then he reached for her hand again. "Can we pray?" He prayed a beautiful prayer, thanking God for the food, asking Him to make it nourishment for their bodies, and thanking Him for their relationship and that it would bring glory to God.

Polly cut her fish sandwich in half and picked it up. And stared at it.

With a slight teasing tone in his voice, Jim asked,

"Don't you want to go to the salad bar first?"

She looked up and he was grinning. The connection was there but it wasn't all consuming anymore.

She grinned back. "Yes! I'm actually hungry now."

When they finished eating, he said "I had a professional motive for asking you out too, not just a personal one. Although I confess that's the main reason I wanted to see you."

"Oh?"

"We got the autopsy report today. It turns out that Tom Broughton wasn't killed by a blow to the head."

"He wasn't?" She took a sip of water.

"Nope. You ready for this? He died of drowning."

"Drowning? In his kitchen?"

"Doesn't look like he died in the kitchen. More like in his bed. He had a lot, a whole lot, of a drug called Cyclobenzeprine HCL in his system. It's a muscle relaxant. It also showed that there had been a strong adhesive, like would come from professional strength duct tape, around his mouth and wrists. And there were some marks on his neck that matched the rope noose we found under the kitchen table."

Polly was almost speechless. "Noose? I didn't know about a noose. But what about the gash on his head?"

"Made after death."

"Boy! Talk about overkill!"

Jim threw back his head and laughed. "If that expression ever fit a real crime, it's this time."

Polly shook her head. "I don't understand. Somebody must have really hated him."

"The best I can figure out, he was drugged to a point that, even if he woke up when his attacker came, he wouldn't have any strength. Then his mouth was taped shut, wrists taped together just to make sure he couldn't fight, and water was poured down his nose some way. I'd think probably a small funnel. Then when he was dead, the tape was removed and the body drug out of the bed and into the kitchen with the noose. Then the noose was thrown on the floor, the tape disposed of, and the corpse hit in the head with a heavy blunt object."

"But why? It's sounds like something out of a silly movie."

"Exactly." He had a very serious look on his face. "Is there anything in that game you play that would suggest any of those methods or instruments?"

She shook her head and then stopped. Surely not.

"What? You've thought of something."

"Nothing really. It's just that him being taken into the kitchen made me think of ... it's silly really. We were deciding who best fit the characters in the Victim game and when it came to the Cook, we agreed on Sam Molloy. He brings weird concoctions to the pot-lucks. And well, I wouldn't think anything of it except ... " And she repeated the conversation with Sam after the visitation earlier that evening. "But what would be his motive? I never saw Tom personally attack him in any way. And besides ... I, I like Sam." She finished lamely.

"Anything else?"

"No, not that I can think of." And there wasn't.

Jim took money from his wallet and left a tip on the table.

"Ready to go?"

She wasn't, but she nodded and followed him to where he paid the check. That was uncomfortable. As a sheriff he couldn't make very much. And she had a lot of money. Money from the divorce settlement, money from the house sale. But she couldn't insult him by insisting on paying.

He followed her to her car and opened the door for her. "Mind if I get in the passenger seat for just a minute or two?"

"Sure. I mean I don't mind at all. Please get in for a minute or two." *Or for the rest of our lives.*

When he was settled, he looked at her again. "This is really something. I thought what I felt for you in junior high was a silly childhood crush. Used to make me mad that it spoiled other relationships for me. I guess I daydreamed about you so much that no reality could meet up to it. I've repented for that. And I tried to be a good husband. God's forgiven me for the daydreams and for not being able to love my wife the way a husband is supposed to. I figured that's why she fell in love with someone else and left me." He looked away.

When he paused Polly wasn't sure if she was supposed to say something. But he went on before she could think of anything.

"But when I heard you moved back to Frankfort, it all came back, the need that I tried to ignore. I even tried putting it on other women. I knew I was being ridiculous. But then I saw you. And we talked. And I knew for sure."

Polly's voice was weak, but the words came. "Knew what?"

"That you were the one. This love I have for you is from God. But I have wanted you so long that I'm afraid. Afraid of my own feelings. Afraid that I'll rush you before you are ready. Afraid something will happen to ruin our relationship. I want ... "

Calm poured through Polly like a warm lotion. This time she slid her hand into his. She couldn't believe such boldness came from her. "Look at me?"

He looked at her, a question in his eyes.

"Jim, I've never had these feelings in my life. I've never really loved anybody, not the way a woman is supposed to love a man. My marriage was a farce. I tried but nothing worked. I didn't know 'til this past few weeks what I was supposed to feel. I didn't know that there was 'the one' that God chose for us. But I know now." His hand tightened on hers but he didn't say anything.

"So what now? What does God want from us, for us?"

His response was to pray. "Lord, you have given us this love for each other. Please keep it pure. We give You our future. In Jesus Name, Amen."

He squeezed her hand and then withdrew his. "May I kiss you? Just on the cheek? I don't trust myself with anything more."

She nodded, swallowing the lump in her throat. He leaned over, kissed her softly on the cheek, said goodnight, and left the car.

When she got back to the camper, she let herself in as quietly as possible, hoping Sandy was asleep. She could see a light under the door to the bedroom, but her friend could be reading.

Polly was not ready to answer questions.

On the table there was a notice.

"The funeral for Tom Broughton will be held at Rogers Funeral Home, Second Street, in Frankfort at 3 p.m. on Sunday, instead of RiversEdge Campground."

Chapter Fourteen

Polly laid the paper back on the table when a knock came on the camper door. It was Brenda Croft.

"Hey, hope you don't mind me coming over. I was watching for your car."

Polly could tell her friend was very disturbed about something. "What's wrong?"

"Sandy didn't tell you?" Then she saw the notice lying on the table. "You saw this?"

"Yes. Why are they changing the funeral plans?"

"After you left, there was, a, a ruckus."

Fear flooded Polly's chest. "Sam?"

"No, not Sam. Colonel Wylie."

"What happened? What did he do?"

"He killed himself."

Of all the things Polly was expecting, that was not among them. She sat down on the couch. And pointed Brenda to the place at the other end. "Why? How?"

Brenda shook her head. "Nobody knows why. There was a note that said, 'This is no one's fault but my own.' But no explanation."

Polly hated to ask. "How did he do it?"

"He shot himself in the head. And we all heard the shot. It was Sam who went into the Colonel's camper first. He found him."

Polly groaned. "Oh, how awful for him. They were such good friends. Does Sam have any idea why he did it?"

Brenda shook her head. "If so, he's not saying."

Polly had a horrible thought. "Are you sure he did it himself? Could Sam have done it and just pretended that he found him? That would be easy since they live next door to each other, and their front doors open up to the connected patio."

Brenda looked shocked. "I don't think so. I never thought of such a thing. Why would that even occur you?"

Polly explained Sam's rage about Tom Broughton, and that he'd known that someone else set Dot's camper on fire before the firemen did. "So, what if the Colonel knew Sam was the murderer and confronted him. Sam could have killed him to shut him up."

Brenda shook her head. "I can't imagine Sam Molloy doing any kind of violence."

"He sure was feeling violent at the visitation." Polly shook her head. "And I meant to ask, is Dot still staying with you?"

"No, she moved back to her camper yesterday."

Just then another knock sounded at the door. This time it was Jim.

Feeling a little awkward, Polly said, "Brenda, you remember Jim Murray, the sheriff?" The two exchanged a brief nod.

Jim took Polly's arm. "You know what happened?"

She nodded. "Brenda just told me."

"I left my cell phone in the car during supper, so just got the call." He grinned sheepishly. "I've never done that. Guess I was distracted." Then he looked serious again. "Polly, please leave here. You and Sandy can come to my place for the night."

Polly narrowed her eyes. "Then you think it wasn't suicide?"

Just then Sandy came out of the bedroom, yawning. "What's going on? You all are loud enough to raise the dead."

Polly made a strangled sound in her throat. "I wish."

Jim explained the situation and made his plea again that the two would spend the night at his house. He turned to Brenda. "You too, Ma'am, if you want."

Polly explained. "The sheriff and Sandy are brother and sister. We've all been friends since we were children."

Brenda nodded as if a mystery had been revealed. Polly turned back to Jim. "I can't leave. I'm sorry but I just can't."

He turned to his sister. "Sandy?"

Polly could almost visualize Sandy weighing murder and suicide in one hand and miniature frogs in the other.

"I'm staying with Polly."

Jim sighed. "You stay together, you hear me? And lock the door." He turned back and looked at Brenda. "Ma'am, are you staying, or may I escort you home? I don't think you need to be walking around here alone in the dark?"

"Thank you," Brenda said, and followed him out.

Polly woke up around nine the next morning after a fitful night and very little sleep. Conflicting memories of the night before warred for her attention. Wonderful memories of her time with Jim, horrible thoughts of how Colonel Wylie must have looked shot through the head, heart breaking thoughts of Sam Molloy's feelings if he wasn't guilty. And a sickening realization that her newfound haven could never feel the same again.

She started the coffee pot and headed to the bathroom when her cell phone rang. It was Jim.

"You okay?" At the sound of his voice all the negatives left her.

"Fine. Are you?"

"Yep. I'm coming out there again today. I'll have to miss church. What time is Broughton's funeral?"

"It was going to be one when it was here, but they changed it to three when they moved it to Rogers."

"Are you going?"

"I don't know. I'm going to see Dot and play it by ear - see if she needs me."

"Okay, I plan to be out there around ten. Can you work it out for me to interview in the shelter house again?"

"Sure. At least I'll try. But I can't see any reason why not."

"Okay, see you at ten." But he didn't say goodbye. After a short pause, "Polly?"

"Hmm?"

"I love you."

"I love you too, Jim."

Just as she broke the connection, she heard an exultant, "I knew it!"

Sandy was in the hallway grinning at her.

She grinned back. "You always were a good Nancy Drew."

Polly was about to pass the office on her way to Dot's camper when she spotted her through the window.

"Hey." She closed the door behind her. "I was gone last night and didn't know about the Colonel 'til late. I'm so sorry."

Dot looked up from the counter where she was making notations in a record book. She looked like she'd aged fifteen years in the past week. "Awful. Just awful."

"Do you need me to drive you in to the funeral?"

Dot shook her head. "I'm not going." Polly must have shown her surprise because she went on. "Why should I? He was a terrible husband and we weren't even married when he died. And his family has taken over now. And good riddance is all I can say!"

Polly just nodded. "And, uh, Sheriff Murray asked me to see if it would be okay for him to use the shelter house again to interview some of the residents. I guess about Clayton Wylie's death."

Dot shrugged. "Sure. Why not?"

"Have you seen Sam? Or the Rileys?"

Dot shook her head. "No. And don't want to."

Polly understood that Dot was upset but her attitude toward others who must be grieving too, surprised her.

"Sheriff Murray will be here around ten."

Dot just nodded, head deep in her ledger again.

When Polly left the office, she turned right and could see Lucy and George Riley sitting on their patio talking to Sam Molloy. She took a deep breath and headed to their site. They looked up as she approached.

George stood to his feet and offered her his cushioned chair, but she shook her head and gestured to him to sit back down.

"I just came to say that I'm so very sorry about Colonel Wylie. And ask if there is anything I can do?"

All three of them shook their heads. Lucy said, "That's very sweet of you, dear. I'm sure you know how much we will all miss Clayton."

Polly wanted to ask if they knew any reason why the Colonel would take his own life. But there was a limit, and that would be beyond it. She turned to go and then thought she'd warn them.

"I heard that the Sheriff is coming again around ten to talk to people. I guess it's about the Colonel's death." The three nodded, and Lucy said, "Thank you."

Now that the feelings were admitted and the words said, it was hard for Polly not to run up and hug Jim when she saw him pull up and park right beside the campground office. When he saw her standing in the door of the shelter house, he grinned in a way that told her he felt the same way.

When Helen Bailey got out of the passenger side, Polly was able to greet the young woman with sincere welcome. What a difference a day - or a week - made! She had brought the list they were given last week. There was nobody in the shelter house, so Dot's announcement was just to warn those that might be planning on going there. She told them the lower pavilion was available.

When the announcement was over and the Officer dispatched to gather the first set of people, Jim and Polly were left alone.

He smiled down at her. "Hello, gorgeous."

She looked back up at him. "Ditto."

Jim looked shocked and laughed. "That's the first time anybody ever called me gorgeous."

"Ditto again."

His eyes changed from merriment to a deep warmth. "Then everybody in the world is crazy."

"You're prejudiced." Her words came out in a whisper.

The Deputy arrived with a couple that Polly had seen but didn't personally know. And she nodded to them before she left to return to her camper.

It was around twelve-thirty when Jim called to say that he'd gotten another call and would be back later in the day. She was disappointed.

Sandy was smirking when she turned around. "Okay, so I want to hear all about last night."

What could she tell her friend? Sandy would never understand if she tried to explain how much God was in their relationship, or how their relationship was in God.

She shrugged her shoulders. "You were right. We're in love. Don't know how it happened but there it is!" Polly laughed. "I started to say that it seems like I've known him all my life, but that's no great revelation, is it?"

"So did you kiss and stuff?" Sandy looked eager for details.

"He very properly kissed me on the cheek. No stuff!"

"How disappointing. But then I'd forgotten Jim's a religious fanatic now."

Polly felt like somebody had hit her in the chest. "No, it's not like that. It's respect and integrity."

Sandy threw up both hands. "What do they say on TV - the kids I mean? Oh yeah. My bad!"

Polly had to laugh. Over lunch they discussed the latest development in the murder.

"Do you really think the murder and suicide are connected?" Sandy asked.

Polly shared her discussion with Brenda the night before. "What if Sam is the murderer and Clayton Wylie knew it and Sam killed him to keep him quiet?"

"Or what if Clayton Wylie was the murderer and killed himself because he didn't want to get caught."

Polly stared at her friend in admiration. "I never thought of that!" She pursed her lips. "Hmm, what if Sam knew it and that's why he was so upset this past few days and was so angry at the visitation?"

"Makes sense to me." Sandy looked pleased with herself.

"And the Colonel was on that list we found in

Broughton's camper. Wonder what he was being blackmailed about?"

"But don't forget Bill Trent. He was on the list too and had the additional motive of his wife's relationship with Broughton."

Polly sighed. "In the mystery books there is always something really obvious that comes out to point them to the killer. Of course, there's also always some scary, dangerous part that comes near the end. I'd just as soon skip that!"

"Yeah, me too."

They were still talking about the different suspects when Brenda arrived at the camper again.

"Well, guess what's happened now?"

"What?"

"Jill Trent. She was on her way to the funeral when she had a wreck. She's in the hospital. Nothing bad but they are going to keep her overnight and watch for concussion symptoms. They're pretty sure she has one."

Polly wished Brenda wasn't telling them the news with such relish. She seemed almost glad about it.

"But the exciting part is this: they took the car to the garage where Doug works, and he called and told me. The front left brake line had been cut!"

"Oh!" This was a shock. Jill Trent. How many victims were there in this campground situation? She wondered if Jim knew about this latest. Well, he would in a minute.

She called his cell phone but there was no answer. She could feel herself blushing. He was on duty and probably thought she was calling personally. So she left a message. "Just wanted to let you know there's a new development at the campground. Another tragedy, or almost tragedy."

Polly didn't see Jim until six that evening when he knocked on the camper door. He told her the garage where Doug Croft worked contacted him before he got a chance to hear her message. When he showed up at her camper, he told them he came out around four and did more investigations. Deputy Sanders drove the other patrol car, so she could leave when their investigations were done, and he could come there to be with them.

"We're awfully glad you did. You look exhausted. Stretch out on the couch and rest. And we'll figure out something for supper." Polly fluffed out some pillows and Sandy moved the book she'd laid there.

Jim didn't even argue. They didn't ask any questions and within five minutes, he was snoring. Not a loud snore.

Sandy looked at Polly and spoke softly. "I think you could live with that!"

Polly looked down at the sleeping sheriff as waves of something - tenderness? - flooded her body. "Yes, definitely I could live with that."

They went outside and sat at the chairs around the round metal table there on the patio. It was a nice evening, warm but with a slight breeze blowing. One of those times when if it wasn't for the breeze you wouldn't notice the weather at all. Just about perfect skin temperature. Polly's favorite kind of climate.

"Oh, Sandy. So much joy and so much confusion right now. I feel like my emotions are in the middle of a storm."

"Just think, Polly, you and I will become real sisters."

"He hasn't asked me to marry him, Sandy. We've only been reconnected five days. This would seem insane to anybody but the three of us."

"But we don't care what anybody else thinks, do we?

Polly gave her friend a grateful smile. "No we don't. I'm still in a state of shock. I didn't know you could feel so connected to anybody." Then a thought occurred to her. "Is this the way you felt about Kyle? The way you and he were toward each other?"

She saw tears spring to her friend's eyes as she nodded.

"I'm sorry, Sandy. I had no idea. No wonder you've been so miserable since he died."

"I knew you didn't understand, Polly. And how could you, all those years with Walter?"

"Well, I'm still sorry that I wasn't more sympathetic. Forgive me?"

"Of course. Friends forever."

"Friends forever."

Chapter Fifteen

When Jim woke up, they heated up some ham and cheese for sandwiches and opened a package of Frito's. Sandy made a pot of coffee for herself; Jim and Polly had bottles of water.

He frowned. "I thought you liked coffee, Polly. Don't give it up on my account."

"I never drink coffee after four in the afternoon. Don't want it to keep me up."

Sandy added, "That's true. She never will. I, on the other hand, drink it clear up 'til bedtime and it never fazes me."

"Okay, Ladies. Tell me what you think is going on. Who would purposefully cause an accident to Jill Trent?"

The two women exchanged glances.

Polly answered. "Since I don't know whose husband Jill is after now, I couldn't guess." Then contrition hit her. "I'm sorry. I shouldn't have said that. But, Jim, the woman has no shame. She is after men and doesn't care who she hurts. She's sarcastic and puts people down. The only good thing I can say about her is that she is a really great blues singer." After a few seconds of musing, she added, "The Musician."

Jim cocked his head to one side. "The Musician?"

Polly laughed briefly. "Dot and Brenda and I played Victim a lot last week and once we were trying to decide who at the campground fit the different roles of the game. Remember, I told you we called Sam the cook? We voted that Jill is the musician."

"Okay. Who were the others?" Jim looked like he was really interested.

Polly sent her mind back to that Friday. Was it really just a week ago tomorrow? Her entire life had changed in less than a week.

"Let's see. We all agreed that George and Lucy Riley were the Banker and the Artist. The Soldier was Clayton Wylie, Jill was the Musician and her husband Bill, the Salesman. We labeled Tom Broughton the Handyman." She gave a short laugh. "Brenda and I thought Dot was the perfect Secretary, but she didn't see it, so we gave that role to Helen Gabbard." She closed her eyes. "I remember we were discussing who would be the most likely victim when the argument between Tom Broughton and the Riley's interrupted our talk. Dot got up to go pour cool water on the flames." She purposefully didn't quote Dot's comment on wishing they could choose the Victim. "What made you ask about that?"

Jim scratched his head. "Oh, I don't know. Sometimes those things can be revealing. You know, people's subconscious opinions surfacing."

Polly laughed. "Sorry. There wasn't much subconsciousness about our discussion."

He pushed his chair back and stood up. "Ladies, it's been great. Thank you for supper - and the nap. I really better go now."

Polly's stomach dropped. "I was hoping you could stay."

He looked down at her and the connection happened again. "I want to. But I can't."

Polly felt like she might faint right then and there. This was ridiculous. She wondered how soon he would propose. How soon she could talk him into getting married? At the same time another part of herself was telling her she was crazy.

It wasn't very long after Jim left that Brenda showed up at the camper. "You all want to play cards or Victim or something?"

Polly looked at Sandy.

"You go on," her friend said. "I've got a book I'm reading."

Polly walked with Brenda down to the shelter house. "Have we heard any more about how Dot is? And anything about the Colonel's funeral?"

"Nothing about Dot. Sam Molloy is supposed to be handling the funeral. Seems he was the executor of the Colonel's will or something."

There were very few people at the shelter.

"How about Gin Rummy?" Polly suggested.

"Perfect for two," agreed Brenda.

They got cards out of the game box and cut for the deal. Polly got it and began dealing the cards.

"Oh, by the way," Brenda said, "I sold the Mind

Games game."

"Really?"

"Yes, for $40 plus shipping. On e-bay. Sure you don't want me to split with you?"

"Positive." Polly had never let anyone know how well off she was. She didn't want to be treated differently. A thought struck her. Would her money make a difference to Jim? Oh, surely not!

Brenda was talking. "And she owns a collectables store in Christchurch, New Zealand. Isn't that neat?"

"Yes, I like how, because of the internet, we can connect with people on the other side of the world." She would not sit and worry about Jim. She would pay attention to her friend and the card game.

"Her name is Lindsay Wilson. Spelled with an a. I told her we have a college here in Kentucky with her name, only spelled with an e - Lindsey Wilson College in Columbia."

After a few games, Brenda's cell phone rang.

"Be there as soon as this game is over." She turned to Polly. "Doug's on his way home. See you tomorrow? Are you coming to the line dancing tomorrow night?"

"Are they still having it? After all the deaths and everything?"

Brenda nodded. "Most of the weekenders won't be affected at all. And a lot are coming just for that event."

The four people at the other table were putting their cards away and folding up chairs so Polly waited. Brenda told her how to lock the shelter and where to hide the key for whoever would unlock in the morning. When they had all left, Polly closed up and headed back to her camper.

She'd never walked back at night when the lights were off in the shelter house. It felt a little eerie. It occurred to her that Jim would not be happy at her being here alone. "You stay together, you hear me?" he'd said to Sandy and her. And to Brenda, "You don't need to be walking around here alone in the dark."

She shook off the creepy feeling. There was nothing to be afraid of. But why was it so very dark? She knew she'd turned her outdoor light on when she left. But no, her camper was completely dark. She could barely see it's outline.

She stepped lightly onto the patio, making sure she held onto the table so she wouldn't stumble ...

"Polly, Polly! Somebody help!" Sandy was bending over her, yelling, and lights were coming on in the neighboring campers.

She shook her head, "What happened?"

"Oh, thank God!" Sandy hugged her. "I was asleep and heard this clattering and got up to look, the outside light was out so I turned on the living room one, and there you were. Lying on the ground, passed out."

Polly struggled to sit up, just as several men rounded the camper, one of them Doug Croft.

"Ms. Nichols, are you okay?"

"I'm fine." Polly shook her head in an attempt to shake off the clouds in her brain.

"No, she's not," Sandy insisted. "She was knocked completely out."

"But I'm okay now. I promise. What happened?"

Doug turned a flashlight toward the concrete floor

of the patio. There beneath a chair that had fallen over was what looked like part of a sawed-off tree, about a foot tall and two feet wide.

"Where on earth did that come from?" Sandy sounded indignant.

"Did you have that here, Ma'am, as a stool or decoration?" A man Polly didn't know asked the question in a kind voice as Sandy helped her to her feet.

"No, I never saw it before."

Brenda Croft joined them, dressed in a robe. "What on earth?"

"She tripped over that," her husband pointed to the wood piece. Then he turned to Polly. "I really think you should go to the ER and let them check you out, Ma'am. Since you were unconscious and all."

"Yes!" Sandy agreed. "I'll drive her in to the hospital."

They were still in a little room, a roomlet as Polly called it, when a familiar face peered around the opening.

"Jim!"

He hurried in and patted Sandy on the shoulder. But he leaned over Polly and kissed her forehead and took her hand and held it to his lips.

"What did they say?"

Polly gave a little laugh. "They haven't even been in yet." She gave Brenda a stern look. "You called him?"

"Of course she did," Jim answered. "I'd have kicked her if she hadn't."

Polly couldn't really be angry. It was so good, so safe, so right to have him here. She thought she could go to sleep now. She took his hand and held it to her cheeks and closed her eyes.

"No, Sweetheart, you need to stay awake."

Just then the medical staff came in, whisked her away, did some kinds of tests, and then brought her back to where Jim and Sandy were waiting. Home. From now on, Polly knew wherever Jim was would be home to her. And her very best friend was an extra bonus.

In a shorter time than they expected, the ER doctor came back with the good news that absolutely nothing was wrong, no concussion, no broken bones, nothing sprained.

"But you will probably be sore for a few days. If you can bathe in hot Epsom Salts, it will help."

Then brother and sister took her out to Sandy's car. Jim followed them to Wal-Mart where he went in and got Ibuprofen and Epsom Salts while they waited in the car.

When he came out he had Polly roll down the passenger window and handed her the bag of supplies. "Please come and stay at my house."

But Polly did not want this to be the occasion on which she first spent the night at Jim Murray's home.

He followed them to the campground and made sure they were locked in. Doug Croft had already screwed in the light bulb which was loosened.

With another warning to stay together, stay locked in, and to call him in the morning, he left. From the window, Polly watched the patrol car until it was out of sight.

They didn't wake up until after ten o'clock and

Sandy refused to let Polly get off the couch except to go to the bathroom.

"I feel fine," Polly complained. "That Epsom salts bath did the trick. Seriously."

"That may be, but it's not going to hurt you to rest. Now call Jim and let him know how you are."

Polly didn't mind that order at all. And she didn't mind the eagerness of the voice that answered the phone call.

"I'm fine," she said softly. "Thank you so much for coming last night. I ... I do love you!"

"About time!"

She smiled, even though he couldn't see her. "So when will I see you again? Tonight?"

"I couldn't come for a social event out there with unsolved cases still open, even if I weren't already committed for tonight. No, I'm afraid it will have to be tomorrow."

Disappointment swept over her. "Oh."

"I'm really sorry, Sweetheart, but I promised a friend from high school who's coming in to visit his parents that I'd have supper and spend the evening with him and some other guys from my class. I don't think you'd know him, or them. We were the obnoxious younger kids back then."

It was ridiculous to resent this unknown person who was taking Jim's time away from her. Whoa, she'd better watch it. Jealousy and possessiveness were not what she wanted to feel or act on.

"I hope you have a wonderful time with your friends, Jim. And I'll be looking forward to seeing you tomorrow."

That night, Polly talked Sandy into going down to the lower pavilion with her. The musicians were going to be there. "After all that's why you were staying over, right?"

"Okay, but we're driving."

They packed two lawn chairs into Sandy's trunk and arrived just as the band started playing. Brenda's face lit up and she motioned them to sit beside her.

When they were all settled, she said, "I wanted to see you but was afraid to bother you. Sheriff Murray stopped by last night and told us you were okay but would probably need a lot of rest today. He's so nice."

Polly smiled and said, "Yes, he is." If Sandy weren't there, she would probably tell Brenda what was going on with her and Jim. Just like an eighth grader. But, that's okay, she told herself. Love definitely youthens!

The line dancing was entertaining to watch and finally when they did the "Hokey Pokey" just for fun, Polly couldn't stand it. "I'm going. Come with me?"

Sandy declined but Brenda joined her. Put your right foot in, put your right foot out. Anybody could get it right dancing to the Hokey Pokey. No matter how clumsy. Walter used to tell her that she was so clumsy she should never try to dance. But she loved dancing and the Hokey Pokey seemed made for her. Walter would not have been surprised at her fall last night.

Polly shook the thought of Walter off as she stuck her "right hand in and shook it all about." He had no more power to make her feel clumsy or stupid or any other way. The most wonderful, handsome, kind, amazing man in the world loved her!!! She had to admit the exercise made her head hurt a little bit, but not much. And the fun was worth it.

As they were walking back to their chairs, Brenda whispered to her. "I really want to talk to you."

"Without Sandy around?"

"I don't think it matters. I just want us to brainstorm about all this ... all these victims." And Brenda stared at her in the eyes, like she was trying to convey some deep meaning.

"Would you like to come over for coffee in the morning? We could call you when we get up?"

Brenda sighed. "Yes, I'd like that very much." The look in her eyes troubled Polly.

When the three women were settled around her table the next morning, coffee cups filled in front of them, Polly turned to Brenda. "Okay, what's up?"

Brenda immediately frowned. "Do you remember the night before Jim's death - when we were playing Victim and Bill Trent joined us?

"Sure." Polly nodded and turned to Sandy. "He's the husband of Jill Trent, the one we suspect was having an affair with Tom Broughton. Tom had invited people down to the lower pavilion to have a good time, implying that we were boring, just playing games. He especially looked at Jill."

"Do you remember what bad luck Bill had?"

Polly turned to Sandy again. "He lost in an amazingly short time and said, "Guess I'm just a natural victim tonight, huh?'"

Brenda looked directly at Polly. "Do you remember

what those three losses, that made him the Victim, were?"

Polly cast her mind back a week to that game. "Hmm. I remember there was a fire. And I remember praying, I know it's silly, but I felt so sorry for him. Oh!" She looked at Brenda in horror. "He lost by tripping over a stump."

Brenda nodded triumphantly. "Exactly! He had a fire. He had an automobile accident, and he tripped over a stump. Remind you of anything?"

Polly was stunned. "Dot had a fire in her camper, Jill had an automobile accident, and I tripped over a stump!" She was silent a few seconds, thinking over the implications. "And none of them were really accidents. Dot doesn't smoke, Jill's brake line was cut, and I didn't have a stump on my patio when I left that night." She shook her head. "Who on earth? It had to be Bill who did those things." She shuddered.

"No wonder Jim wanted us out of here," Sandy said. "I'm calling him now!"

Chapter Sixteen

It didn't take Jim long to get to RiversEdge and soon the four of them were seated around the table.

"Okay, girls. Tell me again what happened."

Polly pointed to Brenda who went over the game that Friday night. "But why would he reproduce those in real life? Surely he knows we would remember? And why would he want to do that anyway? I mean, okay, we can see why he'd be angry at Jill. And if he was mad enough to kill Tom, why not try to get rid of her? But ... "

Polly interrupted. "But why cause an accident to Dot or me? Just to make it look like Jill wasn't the only intended victim?" She shook her head.

"Okay, ladies." Jim scratched his head. "It's true that Bill Trent does have a shadowy past. He's been fortunate enough - or tricky enough - not to be arrested on any felony charges. But I'm very leery of him. The threat found in Broughton's camper really doesn't seem like his MO. And we don't know how old the note is. It could have been written by anybody. So that isn't influencing my thinking, but his name on the list is. It is very probable that Broughton was in the blackmailing business. My investigation shows that a liquor store owner in a nearby county has the nickname Sal and a reputation for selling to minors. But the other two - the Colonel and Trent are here at the campground. I have no doubt that the motive for Wylie's suicide is the blackmail. But was it because he murdered Broughton, or was he afraid the blackmail information would come out?"

Polly shook her head slowly. "I guess I'm really gullible. I felt so sorry for Bill Trent, the way his wife just went off with Tom. And you could tell he really did feel like a loser. Or that's what I thought."

"Okay, let's look at this a little more closely. Who was around that could have heard what was going on in your game? People watching, or playing at a nearby table?"

Polly and Brenda looked at each other, each biting their bottom lip.

Brenda spoke first, "The Riley's and Sam and Col. Wylie left because of Tom insulting the Colonel."

Polly added, "And then when Tom suggested partying at the lower pavilion, the rest didn't take long to follow. We were alone. Just Dot and you and me, and Bill. It had to be him."

Brenda suddenly sat up straight. "Or you. Or me." She paused. "Or Dot."

Jim pushed his chair back. "Okay that does it. I want all of you out of here now. Mrs. Croft, where is your husband?"

"He's working this morning."

"Call and tell him you're going with Sandy and Pol-ly."

"Yes, Sir." She pulled out her cell phone.

Jim worked a key off of his key ring and handed it to Polly. "Go into town, eat lunch, shop, do whatever you want to do and go to my house when you're through. Keep your cell phone on." He grinned for a second. "Don't call me. I'll call you."

Polly put her hand on his arm. "Be careful."

He bent over and kissed her on the forehead. "You too, my love."

Polly could see him watching them from in front of the office as they pulled out of the campground. Sandy was driving, and Brenda was in the front seat while she stared out of the back window. "Lord, please keep him safe," she whispered.

None of them felt like shopping or eating so they went straight to Jim's house.

"Oh, how pretty!" Brenda's eyes widened when she saw the house and yard. "Who would have thought of a Sheriff living in a place like this?"

Polly unlocked the door and they followed her in-side. Sandy turned back and shot the dead bolt.

"Now what?" Polly asked. "What do we do while we wait?" When the others didn't answer, she asked, "Would it be okay, could we pray?"

"Sure," Brenda said. "Well, you can. I don't pray out loud."

"Go for it!" Sandy agreed.

Polly wasn't used to praying out loud either but there didn't seem to be a choice. She bowed her head and put her hands together.

"God, we need you to help. Help us and help Jim. I

think I heard that you send angels to protect people. Will you do that for Jim? And show him what really happened all this last week. And make all the bad things stop. And keep Jim safe. And everybody else too. And God, if ... if Dot did these bad things, we ask you to help her be sorry and help her come to you for help. And if Bill did them, we ask the same thing. Amen. I mean, in Jesus' Name, Amen." She breathed a sigh of relief when she said the last Amen.

She was surprised when Brenda echoed, "Amen."

And shocked when Sandy did the same.

She was staring at Sandy when her friend addressed Brenda. "My little brother's kind of a religious fanatic. I think our Polly is going to have to learn a new way of life when she moves in here!"

Brenda turned to Polly. "I was surprised back at your camper when he called you 'my love.' I didn't know."

Polly laughed and shook her head. "I didn't either. I mean, we hadn't seen each other for decades and to me, he was just Sandy's little brother. But it seems he had a crush on me when he was in junior high that never quite went away. And, well, I seem to have caught it."

Brenda clapped her hands. "How romantic." But then she made a grimace. "But I don't want you to move here."

Polly shrugged her shoulders. "You know I never thought about moving in here." She turned to Sandy. "He hasn't asked me to marry him and you know we're not going to just live together. I may never live here." But she had a funny feeling inside that she was, at this moment, sitting in her future home.

Then she turned to Brenda. "But even if that happens, I know I'd keep the camper. I love it. And I love being there." She paused. "Well, once the murderer is caught, I'll love being there again."

Brenda smiled and patted her arm. "Good, we need you."

"Will you really be able to live with all these animals and go to that church?" Sandy questioned Polly.

"The church I really believe I'll have no problem with. And for your baby brother, I can get used to the menagerie." Polly said as she stroked the Cocker Spaniel who lay with his head against her leg. She looked over at the large aquarium that stood against the wall. "They say watching fish swim is very calming and therapeutic." The cat was asleep in the guest bedroom and the other dog was out in the yard. "The animals all seem very well trained. "I haven't seen the frogs."

"Oh, I asked him. He doesn't have them anymore."

Polly didn't mind admitting that she was glad about the frogs.

They finally got hungry and decided to go to Appleby's for soup and salad. Polly ordered her favorite - French onion soup and oriental salad. She used to get the pecan crusted chicken salad, but they quit carrying it and she still missed it. The other two got Tomato Bisque and oriental salad. It was nearly three when they got back to the house.

Polly had just locked the door behind them when her cell phone rang. It was Jim.

When she disconnected, she turned to the others. "Okay. He wants us to stay here, Sandy. And Brenda, he wants you to have Doug call him." Brenda wrote down Jim's cell phone number and stepped into the kitchen to call her husband.

"He said for us to make a list, Sandy, and he'll get whatever we want from the camper and bring it. And he's going to talk to Doug about getting some stuff for Brenda. He says the two of us, Brenda and I, are the two in the greatest danger right now. I don't know who from, Dot or Bill.

"Wow. This got serious, didn't it. Too big for Nancy Drew."

"Or Judy Bolton." Polly sighed.

It was around six when Doug Croft came for Brenda and took her off to Lexington to stay in a hotel for the weekend. Shortly afterwards, Jim came home, with the things from the lists Polly and Sandy had given him. "I didn't tell anyone anything. If they wonder where everybody is, they just wonder." He looked around and tugged at his collar. "Look, I could take you two to a hotel too, or send you to Louisville, but it sure would make me more comfortable if you stayed here 'til Monday."

"Monday? Why Monday?" Sandy frowned at him.

"I should have all the information I need to make an arrest by then. Forensics promised they'd have it all ready by noon on Monday."

Polly searched Sandy's face. Praying her friend would accept the offer. She couldn't stay here alone with Jim and she really didn't want to go to a hotel or Sandy's house.

Sandy must have read her unspoken plea. "Okay, we'll stay."

Joy flooded Jim's face. "Great. I'll go out and pick up something for supper. What do you want?"

"I want Chinese," his sister said.

"Does that suit you, Jim?" Polly tried not to look adoringly at him, but that was how she felt.

"Absolutely." He went to the kitchen and came back with a menu. "I'll call it in and can pick it up in ten minutes."

"You mean, you don't already know what we want?" Polly teased him. " Moo Goo Gai Pan for me, white rice, and two vegetable spring rolls."

"Chicken with broccoli, fried rice, and egg rolls." Sandy laid down the menu. "And what do you want, Little Brother?"

"I always get sweet and sour chicken. And fried doughnuts."

Polly spoke before she thought. "That can't be healthy!" She felt herself blushing. "I'm sorry. I didn't mean to be critical."

"That's why God said, 'It's not good for man to be alone.'" He laughed and called in the order on his way out the door.

Sandy opted to stay home from church that Sunday, but Polly gladly went with Jim. This time she enjoyed it even more, not having to worry about what her friend was thinking about the service.

Before they left the parking lot, Jim turned to her. "Think you could get used to this church?" He did that eye connection thing again.

Even though she felt like she was drowning, she

managed to nod.

Jim turned the motor off and ignored all the cars exiting around them. "Polly, this is so quick. We've only been seeing each other for eight days. And I know you're still grieving over the breakup of your marriage."

She stopped him short. "Absolutely not. There was never any grief. I feel free for the first time in my life. That's probably the reason I've insisted on my own way and refused to leave the campground until I knew it was time. I've been controlled and put down and run around on all my married life. I have not felt one tiny bit of grief. And I have had no love for Walter for decades. It was not hurtful that he left me."

She grinned. "Especially since he thought I would be upset and offered me an extremely generous settlement as well as the house." Then as an afterthought she added, "Which I sold." She looked away. "That's the only thing I've worried about, Jim. About our relationship, I mean. I have an awful lot of money. Does that make you feel uncomfortable?"

With a very serious look on his face, he began patting his ear, his head, his arm, his leg, his stomach. Just as Polly was beginning to wonder if something was wrong with him, he said, "Nope, can't find a single uncomfortable feeling."

Polly let out a horselaugh. A very unladylike horselaugh. She could feel the blush spread over her face. "I'm sorry."

"I'm glad. I meant to make you laugh."

Then the eye connection thing happened again. "Polly, I love you. I've always loved you. I want to marry you and I want to do it as soon as possible. I feel like so many years have been wasted." This time he looked away. "Do you think I'm crazy?"

She reached up, touched his cheek, and gently turned his face back toward hers. "No crazier than I am."

With that, he pulled her toward him and kissed her. Not on the cheek this time.

It was noon on Monday when Polly's cell phone rang, and Jim said she and Sandy could come back to the campground. The murderer was in the county jail. And he was sure Polly could be of help at the campground. He'd driven back out there after the arrest to gather the residents and let them know what had happened, but he'd like Polly to be there.

She and Sandy arrived within thirty minutes.

The campground owners were gathered in the shelter house, all with very serious countenances. When Polly saw Bill and Jill Trent sitting at a table holding hands, she knew.

"Dot Broughton killed her ex-husband," Jim announced. "It was really bizarre and if any of you want to leave before I go further, you may." Nobody moved. So, he went on.

"We may never know why she did it the way she did it. But she drugged him first, looks like pills crushed and put in a beer, made sure he was passed out, taped his wrists and mouth, and poured water down his nostrils until he drowned."

He looked around at the group. Polly could see that none of them were about to leave.

"Then she wrapped a noose around his neck and

drug him from the bed to the kitchen floor. And as if that wasn't enough, she took a wrench and hit him on the head. That was where she made her first mistake. The second mistake was hiding the wrench in the junk pile behind the office where the pieces of tree limbs are kept for the fall and early winter bond fires. When Polly tripped over the wood, I went looking for its source and found the wrench. Dot Broughton's fingerprints were on the handle and DNA from Tom Broughton was on the head of the wrench."

Lucy Riley was the first to speak. "Was it she who caused the accidents? Surely she didn't set her own camper on fire?"

"Yes, Ma'am," Jim replied. "She did. She was reproducing incidents from a game that happened to Bill Trent when he played Victim with Mrs. Croft, Polly Nichols, and herself. And they were no accidents. She knew she could see her own camper from the office and stop the fire before there was any real damage. And I think she knew Polly wouldn't get seriously hurt. But I also think she would have been happy if Jill Trent's accident had turned out to be fatal." He paused. "But mostly she wanted Bill Trent to be blamed. She admitted planting a threatening note, hoping we'd think Trent sent it."

"I don't understand," Jill's face was drained of all color.

"I do." Her husband raised his head and looked around at the people. "She was jealous because Tom had been after Jill even before their divorce. And ... well it's not very gentlemanly to admit, but recently she'd been coming on to me. And I wouldn't have anything to do with her. So she was going to get rid of eve-

rybody that made her unhappy, everybody that reject-
ed her." He looked over at Polly. "Everybody that made
her feel like a loser."

Lucy Riley lifted her voice again. "But what about
Colonel Wylie. Did she kill him?"

Jim looked at her gently. "No, Ma'am. He killed
himself, just like his note said."

"But why?" The grande dame sounded insistent.

"We may never know the answers to that."

Polly wondered why the blackmail list wasn't mentioned. But since Jim didn't bring it up, she wasn't
going to. She looked over at Brenda who shrugged her
shoulders. Suddenly a flash of memory hit Polly's
mind. She and Brenda were at the puzzle table, and
she said, "Wouldn't it be awful if we worked on this so
long and then found there were some pieces missing?"
She felt like that now.

Soon all the residents drifted away to their own
campers. And Sandy announced that she was going
back to Louisville now that Polly was safe.

Jim and Polly helped her pack her remaining
things and hugged her goodbye. She got in her car and
rolled down the window. "Now don't you two go and
elope or anything. I want to be there."

Jim looked at Polly questioningly. She laughed. "I
didn't say a word."

He put his arm around Polly and hugged her close
to him. "You'll be the first to know, Big Sister."

They watched as she turned the curve and exited
the campground.

They were walking hand in hand back toward Polly's camper when someone behind them cleared their
throat. "Excuse me."

When they turned, it was Sam Molloy. Polly, with her other hand, reached for the older man's hand. "Sam, are you okay?"

"Well no, Ma'am. Not very. But ... " He looked at Jim. "Sheriff, could I talk to you, both of you, somewhere private."

"Come into my camper," Polly offered.

When they were seated around the table, all three of them drinking herbal tea, Sam began.

"I think you have a right to know. Well, maybe I just have a need to tell somebody. And I think you two will understand. I think." He swallowed with visible difficulty. "I hope. I want you to understand about Clay - Colonel Wylie."

Polly could see him clenching his teeth. Trying to keep from crying?

"Wouldn't want anyone else to know this." He looked from one to the other.

"It's a promise, Sam." Polly reached out and took his hand.

Jim nodded.

Sam cleared his throat and went on. "Clay killed himself because he thought I murdered Tom Broughton."

"What?" The exclamation slipped out of Polly's mouth before she knew it was coming.

"Yes, that man has been blackmailing Clay. Even though we never ... " He cleared his throat again. "We weren't lovers, not physically, but he heard us talking one night - and knew how we felt about each other. Clay paid the scum, money he couldn't afford. Money he needed for his medications. I hated Broughton. Would have killed him if I'd had the guts. When it happened I was afraid Clay had done it. And he was afraid I had." He shook his head and Polly saw the tears in his eyes. "That's what he meant when he wrote 'This is no one's fault but my own.' He wanted me to know he didn't blame me. And he wanted others to think he was the murderer." The old man put his head in his hands and sobbed.

After a minute, he wiped his face with a handkerchief pulled from his pocket and blew his nose. "I'm sorry."

Polly laid her hand on his. "Can I ask you a question?" It might be her last opportunity to obtain one small puzzle piece. He nodded.

"How did you know someone purposefully set the fire in Dot's camper?"

"Oh, that was simple. They said she left a cigarette burning but I knew she didn't smoke."

One more person came to the camper after Sam had gone home. Bill Trent knocked on the door and Polly let him in.

"Noticed you were still there, Sir." He looked at Jim. "And I wanted to confess something."

"Do you want me to leave?" Polly asked.

"No, Ma'am. It's okay." He turned back to Jim. "I sure am obliged to you for finding out the real killer. I was just sure I'd be blamed. I had reason, you know. I used to deal drugs in the past and that ... " He glanced at Polly. "That so and so was blackmailing me. See, Jill had a bad childhood, parents were addicts and abusive, and she'd never have anything to do with drug dealers. I'd quit before I met her but ... Broughton knew it and threatened to tell her and say he'd seen me dealing here, unless I paid him money. So I did. Stupid, I know." He held out his hand to Jim. "Thank you, Sheriff. Wanted you to know. I'm not sorry he's gone. Maybe Jill and I can make our marriage work now."

Jim shook his hand. "We'll pray for you, and your marriage."

Bill Trent looked surprised. "Thank you, sir. And you Ma'am. I appreciate it."

When he'd gone, Polly turned to Jim with tears in her eyes.

"How many victims are there out there in the world?"

"More than we can imagine, Sweetheart. But not too many for Jesus to rescue."

And he took her in his arms and kissed her again!!!

Chapter Seventeen

When the alarm went off, Jim woke up grinning. Today was the day. He already asked Polly to have dinner with him at Logan's. What she didn't know was that he was going to propose formally.

Before Sandy left the campground and went home to Louisville, he got her to find out Polly's ring size. And when Polly thought she was leaving Frankfort, his sister had actually agreed to meet him at Selbert's jewelry store on the way out of town to help pick out a ring. And the store had called him yesterday afternoon and said the ring was ready.

He chose Selbert's because it was closing in just a few days and was the only jewelry store left in Frankfort from their childhood. He hoped Polly would love the ring - and the sentiment. He trusted Sandy's taste and that she would know Polly's. It was an interesting visit to the store. Philip Selbert, a former bugle boy in the Civil War, and his wife Mary, founded the first jewelry store in Frankfort in 1872. And artist Paul Sawyer shopped there, and often paid with his paintings. Jim loved the thought that the engagement ring and their wedding rings came from a place with a lot of history.

Jim turned the radio on to Willie's Roadhouse and listened to country music on the way to the sheriff's office, singing along at the top of his lungs! It was his favorite station, mixing romance and funny songs, some of which had been popular back as far as he could remember. And at last he didn't identify with Patsy Cline's 'Crazy'. He was no longer crazy for loving Polly. Soon to be Polly Murray!

His deputies were already at the office when he walked in. Helen Bailey, the City Police Officer called them 'the M and M's', the first M being himself, Murray, the others M's being Morales and Mills.

Oh, he'd have to tell Helen soon about Polly. She'd met Polly while they were investigating at the Campground, but that was before anything had happened between him and the love of his life. He hoped Helen didn't still care about him except as a friend. She was a nice lady and he didn't want to hurt her.

Before he could even greet the deputies, Hank Mills said, "Hey boss, a lawyer called and left a number for you. Said to ask you to call back as soon as possible."

Tony Morales grinned. "Been getting yourself in more trouble with women, Sheriff?"

Jim just glared at him. He'd tell them his good news later.

He didn't have to wait long for Clay Patterson's secretary to put him through.

"Hi, Jim, long time no see."

"Right. What's up, Clay?"

"Well, it's about the McAlpin situation. Remember,

the boy who was selling drugs?"

Jim felt his chest tighten. He couldn't keep the disgust out of his voice. "At his mother's insistence!"

"I know. And am totally sympathetic. But there's a problem. The boy doesn't seem like he belongs in detention, especially since it will put him in with a lot of real criminal types. And Child Protective Services got in touch with me."

"Why? Do they want you to go to court for him? Get him declared not guilty?"

"No. They contacted me because somebody in their office knew that we are friends. They asked me to contact you."

"Why? What for?" Jim wasn't sure how his voice sounded but both his deputies turned and stared at him.

"They want him put in foster care, but it really needs to be somewhere that there is the possibility of permanence. There's no way the mother would get him back, even if they find her."

Jim couldn't find his voice. He knew what was coming.

"When they talked to the boy, he asked if he could come and live with you."

Jim swallowed but he couldn't think of any words. Today was his engagement day and he was planning on a fun and carefree life with Polly. But how could he desert Bill? The boy never had anybody that really cared about him, except Jim. Maybe Helen...

"Clay, have they considered Helen Bailey? She really cared for the boy too. And she's a woman. Surely she's a better choice."

"So you want me to tell them no?"

"Well, not yet. Let me pray about it. I'll get back with you tomorrow."

His two silent deputies were waiting patiently as he hung up the office phone.

"Okay guys. I'm going to tell you two things. I'm kind of in a state of shock. I had some good news to tell you. And now I don't know what to do. Maybe one of you has a suggestion."

They looked at him patiently.

Jim sighed. "What I was going to tell you was that I'm getting married." Then he laughed as two mouths literally dropped open.

"I know, but this is a lady I've known since we were kids. She's been my sister's best friend as long as I can remember. I thought it was just a crush; she's three years older than I am. The age mattered when it started; I was in seventh grade and she was a sophomore in high school. But it doesn't make any difference now. And though she never thought of me that way before, well, she does now." His deputies were still silent. "She moved back to Frankfort and now lives at RiversEdge Campground." Both deputies nodded as they realized how the reconnection happened. "Anyway, Polly and I have agreed on marriage. And I have the ring and planned on making a real romantic proposal tonight." He hoped he wasn't blushing.

Mills looked at Morales. "I told you something was going on. Congratulations, Sheriff."

Morales answered, "You were right. Boss, we sure are glad you found a nice lady this time."

"Now here is the problem. Remember the boy we caught selling drugs, and his mother disappeared and left him to take all the blame?"

"Yep," Mills grinned. "You were really hot for her and that hasn't been too long ago."

"Yeah, well, enough about my imbecilic past; I learned my lesson."

"Again," Morales grinned too.

"I know. I deserve all your banter. But this is serious. What Clay wanted is that Juvenile Corrections got him to ask me about being a foster parent for the boy."

They both just nodded, and Jim continued.

"If they had asked before Polly came back, I would have said yes in a minute. But now, what do I do? Polly doesn't know a thing about Billy and I can't ask a sixty-two-year-old woman who never had children to take on an unknown fifteen-year-old boy for three years, and maybe longer. And it certainly would change the marital life I had planned. I can't give her the ring and then ask her about it. And asking her first seems like it would spoil the evening. Any suggestions, guys?" He couldn't believe he was pouring out his thoughts and feelings, but these two were his closest friends. And they were both married with children. Maybe they'd have good suggestions.

"Whoa!" Mills said as Morales groaned.

"Have you prayed about it?" Hank Mills went to the same church that Jim did.

"Well about Polly, yes. But you saw, the situation about Bill just happened. Do you mind...I mean could we pray together now?" Tony Morales was Catholic, and Jim wasn't sure if he believed in private prayer with others.

Before Mills could say a word, Morales spoke. "Definitely! I'll start if you want."

The others nodded, and exchanged a glance of

surprise, and Morales began. "Heavenly Father, You said that Jesus is made unto us wisdom so we are asking that Jesus give Sheriff Jim the wisdom to know what to do in this situation. And please put the boy in the best home for him. Amen."

Mills took over. "Lord, I agree and ask You to guide the Sheriff to know exactly when to talk to his future wife about this. And don't let it hurt their relationship. In Jesus' Name, Amen.

Jim, feeling relieved and like the Comforter Himself was holding him in His arms, continued the prayer. "Father, I don't even know what I want about Billy, but whatever it is, not my will but Thine be done. In Jesus Name, Amen."

Without a word, the three men joined in a group hug.

The trip out to Logan's was wonderful. Polly felt like she was on her first real date ever. The romance in the air enveloped her and she really didn't want to get out of the car. When Jim turned the key off, he looked at her and grinned.

"One kiss before we go in?"

"Yes!" She answered with the enthusiasm of a six-teen-year-old. And the kiss was everything a kiss could be - love, excitement, commitment, oneness. And it was obvious that Jim didn't want it to end any more than she did.

But finally they pulled apart. At his instigation.

He got out of the driver's side and came around to open the door for her. When she got out, she looked up into his face and he leaned toward her. And then pulled away. And laughed. "If I kiss you again, I might never stop."

She grinned at him. "And I certainly wouldn't care."

He laughed. "Then let's get in there quickly!"

The meal was wonderful, medium rare steak. She guessed Jim was as hungry as she was because they both finished everything on their plates. They talked during the meal about their days at Frankfort High School, back when there was no cafeteria and all the students had an hour to eat a lunch brought from home or walk to one of the restaurants a few blocks away.

He was a freshman when Polly and Sandy were seniors, so they never had lunch together but sometimes they'd run into each other at LeCompte and Gayle's, and Sandy would be disgusted that she had to put up with her little brother's presence during the school break. But Polly, who never had any siblings, always smiled warmly at "their little brother."

When dinner was over, Jim looked at her seriously and said, "I've got something I need to talk to you about."

Polly's stomach tightened. *Was he going to say he'd changed his mind? He didn't want to get married? Surely not. Not after that kiss in the car.*

"I've got something to ask you about. It's a big decision we've got to make. And I'm afraid you will have to make it."

We? But I'll have to make it?

"Okay, shoot!" She hoped her voice didn't sound as nervous as she felt.

"I had a case a few weeks ago. Well, it didn't start out as my case. I helped Police Officer Helen Bailey with what looked like an accidental death in town. But then it climaxed out in my territory where a fifteen-year-old kid who was in the car where the accident happened, was selling drugs. But the kid was doing it at his mother's direction. He wasn't happy about it. And it turned out he told about it not being an accidental death. His friend, who was playing detective, was killed by the kids who were really into buying the drugs, some taking, some re-selling, some both. The boy's mother disappeared the day they were caught when she got a call telling her that her son was being held; and she left him. Alone. She had warned him that if he got caught, she would do that because they'd go easy on him. So far she hasn't been found."

Polly just looked at him questioningly.

Jim cleared his throat and took a drink from his water glass on the table.

"Well, the problem is that they don't want to put the boy, who really is a nice kid - his name is Billy - in long term detention and they're looking for a foster home that would be permanent, at least until he's eighteen, three more years."

"And you want to take him?" Her heart was pounding.

"I don't know. I really care about the kid and would have if I was still going to live alone. But I don't want anything to interfere with our marriage life. I wouldn't ask you to take in a strange kid for three years. I've dreamed about us being alone." He grinned. "And what I've dreamed about wouldn't be quite the same with another person in the house."

Polly could feel herself blushing. She thought a minute. "Have you prayed about it?"

"Yes, and got my deputies to pray with me, when the call came in this morning."

Polly smiled. "And?"

"I don't know. I told the Lord I didn't know what I want but that's not the point, I told Him not my will but His be done." He shrugged. "And the only thing that came to me was that you would know His will for us. And for Bill."

"Can I meet him before I make a decision?"

"Of course. But, Polly, which ever you decide, you'll still marry me, won't you?"

"Of course, my love. Nothing on earth could stop me from marrying you, unless you didn't want me."

"That will never happen. Okay then, that's settled. I'll make an appointment for us to go where he is right now in the detention center."

"Good." Polly smiled at him just as the waitress brought the bill.

Jim asked the young woman, "Is it okay for us to stay a few more minutes?"

"Of course. No rush. We don't close for an hour and there are plenty of empty tables if others come in."

When she left, Jim got up from his side of the booth and reached in his pocket. He walked around to Polly's side and shocked her by getting on his knees. He opened the ring box and removed a beautiful diamond and emerald ring.

"Polly Nichols, will you do me the honor of becoming my wife and becoming Polly Murray?"

Her eyes filled with tears. "Yes, yes, a million times yes."

Chapter Eighteen

"I need to talk with you about Billy McAlpin. Want to meet at Captain D's for lunch?" He couldn't go back to Wendy's because of the kiss, and Frisch's belonged to Polly in his mind. Captain D's was the only other fast food place he knew that they both liked.

Helen answered, "Sure but it will have to wait until one. I've got a bunch of paper work and phone calls to take care of."

"That's fine with me."

The deputies were both out of the office, so he picked up his cell phone.

His future wife's voice affected his stomach. "I've got us an appointment with Billy McAlpin, Sweetheart. Tomorrow afternoon at two. That okay?"

"That's perfect. And I really believe after that visit, we'll know what God wants."

"I hope so - and it's in Fayette County so you want to go for lunch first?"

"Of course." And in his mind, he could see the

smile on her face.

"I'll pick you up about 11:30."

He spent the next two hours on his own paperwork and then set out to see Helen.

He spotted her car as soon as she pulled into the parking lot. And sure enough she was seated in a booth waiting for him. He was glad she hadn't bought his lunch again.

"My treat this time. No arguments!" He grinned as he walked up to the booth. "Still want fish and brocco-li? What else?"

Helen gave him a saucy smile. "I'd like corn on the cob but I'm trying to lose a few more pounds so - fish, broccoli, and coleslaw."

Jim nodded and went back to the counter. *That was a little uncomfortable. I think she was flirting. I'll tell her about Polly first thing.*

When he got back to the booth, he set the tray on the table top and sat down. "Mind if I pray?"

Helen shrugged her shoulders. "Okay."

After he said the blessing, he said, "Before we talk about Billy, I want to tell you something. It has to do with him as you'll see." He took a deep breath. "I got engaged to be married last night."

Helen put down the fork full of fish and her mouth dropped. "Married" She shook her head. "Who to?"

"A lady I've known ever since I can remember, since we were kids." He didn't think it necessary to tell that she was older. "You met her. Polly Nichols. She lives at the campground, just moved back to Frankfort from Louisville. She's the one that offered us lunch the day of the murder, but you didn't come."

Helen just nodded. "Well, congratulations. I really

hope you will be happy."

"That - happiness - is the reason I needed to talk to you about Billy." He stopped long enough to eat some fish, a few fries, and take a sip of coca cola.

"It seems that Billy has asked that I become his foster parent if he can get a home parole sentence. "

"Oh, wow. Bad timing."

"Yes, Polly and I are visiting him tomorrow and then we believe we'll know what's the right thing to do. But what I wanted to ask you is, if we believe we shouldn't take him, would you consider it?"

"Absolutely not!" Helen had a look of horror on her face. "I'd never find a husband if I had a teenager in tow, and a criminal one at that!"

Jim was shocked. Helen was not the sweet unselfish person he'd thought she was. He couldn't think of anything to say, so he just nodded.

"Excuse me. I need to go to the bathroom."

While she was gone, Jim finished his lunch. When she came back, he could see a little red around her eyes that made him feel bad.

Helen smiled - but the smile didn't reach her eyes. "I'm going to get a to go box and take this back to the office. I can warm it up in the microwave. Thank you again." She paused. "And I hope everything works out for you and Polly, and for Billy." And she left.

He sighed. *Well, at least that's over. Both issues settled.*

Polly was nervous as she waited on Jim to pick her up. "Lord please, please make Your will for us clear."

She never told Jim how much she'd wanted a child. Walter refused to go to a doctor; of course nothing could be his fault - he was perfect. "Forgive me, Lord. I forgive him, truly I do." She shouldn't think sarcastically about her ex-husband. It was over and done with. She just hoped his new young wife didn't want children. She'd been checked out by several specialists and they could find no reason she couldn't conceive.

But of course it was too late now. And maybe Billy McAlpin was the answer to her decades of prayer. He wasn't an infant but obviously he needed nurturing.

She was looking out the window and saw Jim pull into the campground at 11:29. Very prompt. He would be at her camper exactly at 11:30. She smiled. He was like her. If you say you're going to be somewhere at a certain time, you be there. Her Daddy taught her that if you aren't there when you said, you have lied. And the tone in his voice made it very clear that if you lied, you would go straight to hell. She smiled at the recollection.

The knock on the door interrupted her memories. She grabbed her purse and opened the door. As she started to step out, Jim gently pushed her inside. "Not so fast. We have one thing to take care of before we head out into the public." And he wrapped his arms around her and kissed her.

When he pulled away, Polly said, "We'd better get out of here. Now!" He laughed. "I agree. How soon can we get married?"

As he opened the car door for her, she looked back up at him. "How about eight days?"

The shocked look on his face tickled her. He said, "You mean you'd marry me that soon?

"Sure. Why not?"

"I thought you'd want to do lots of planning and fancy stuff."

"Nope, I'd like to get married here at the pavilion on next Wednesday afternoon. Would you be able to take off for a honeymoon for a while?"

"Yeah. I've got lots of vacation time coming to me. And we're not in the middle of anything."

She nodded. "Well, there's a Bahama Cruise leaving next Friday from Florida. And we'd have time to spend two honeymoon nights on the road and go on the cruise. It's for a week. And then we could mess around Florida a while, maybe go to Disney World and SeaWorld. And I'd love to go back to St. Augustine Beach."

He started the car. "You've really been thinking about this, haven't you?"

She nodded. "That way, we can have some real couple fun before we come back, and you go back to work. And if we become parents, we can get serious about paying lots of attention to Billy."

"Wow. You are going to be the perfect wife. I can already tell."

"I'll book the cruise right now then. I hope they have some cabins left." And she got her cell phone, a notebook, and credit card out of her purse.

When she shut the phone off, she turned to him. "Now we have to get married that soon for sure. Turns out they did have some and we have a seaside suite that was open. I've never been on a cruise and always wanted to."

He glanced over at her. "I would have thought you and Walter..."

She shook her head. "No, he was all business. I did get to go to England once when he had some business over there. And I loved it. That's something else I'd always wanted to do. Since he was working, I got to go places like the Tower of London and Dover Castle all by myself. I loved it." She sighed. "That's why I wasn't at the funeral when your brother-in-law died. We were overseas."

Jim nodded. "Okay, where do you want to eat lunch?"

They decided on Steak and Shake. When they were finished, they got back on the road toward Lexington.

"I'm a little nervous," Polly confessed.

"Why?"

"What if he doesn't like me?"

Jim burst out laughing and reached over to take her hand in his. "Sweetheart, I can't imagine anybody not liking you. What if you don't like him?"

She squeezed his hand. "Jesus is Lord. Right?"

He nodded.

They pulled into the detention center and Jim led them in prayer before they left the car. "Lord, You know what you want for our future, and for Billy's. Jesus is made unto us wisdom and we receive it. And in His name we pray."

To Polly's surprise, they were led into a room and told that Billy McAlpin would be brought to visit with them shortly. That was a relief, no talking through bars or over TV screens.

When the door opened, the teen age boy walked in with a female officer in uniform behind him. When he saw Jim, his eyes lit up. And Jim stood up. He held out his arms and the boy ran into them.

"Hi, son. You okay?"

Jim looked over Billy's shoulder and gave her a sad smile.

The boy's shoulders heaving showed that he was silently sobbing. And Helen knew there was no question about God's will. She'd have her child, even though he belonged completely to Jim right now.

Jim held Billy until he quit crying and then pulled away. "I brought someone I want you to meet, son."

When Jim looked at her she nodded. And smiled. And gave him a thumbs up.

"Billy McAlpin I'd like you to meet Polly Nichols. Polly and I are getting married next week."

The boy smiled at her, a kind of sad smile. "Congratulations, both of you." He turned back to Jim. "Thank you for letting me meet her."

"Well, it's a little more than that, Billy." He grinned. "You two are going to get to know each other a lot in the next few years."

"Huh?" Billy looked at him questioningly.

Jim pulled forth another chair and nodded for the boy to sit down. "Polly and I are getting married and going for an extended honeymoon, maybe as long as a month. But before we leave, we are putting in a petition to the court asking that we become a foster home probation family for you."

Billy's eyes widened as he looked back and forth between the two of them. "You're kidding?"

"No, son. We're not kidding."

Polly got up and went to stand beside Billy and put her hand on his shoulder. "I never had children, Billy, but always wanted one, so you are an answered prayer for me." She smiled as she noted the surprise on Jim's face. She looked back at the teen and his face was radiant.

"Thank you, Ma'am. Thank you so much."

Jim looked at the detention guard. "How much visit time do we have?"

She looked at her watch. "About twenty more minutes."

Polly said, "I want to know what you like to eat so I can have the refrigerator and shelves stocked when you come."

At first Billy just kept looking back and forth between her and Jim. And finally he said. "I like hamburgers and French fries best. And spaghetti. And well, just about anything."

"Well, I'll have all that and then you can go to the grocery with me and help me pick out things."

He nodded. Then he turned to Jim. "Have they caught my mother?"

Jim shook his head. "Not that I know of."

"I won't ever have to live with her again, will I?"

Jim looked at him with great gentleness. "No, son. Never again."

Then they shared with Billy what they were going to do on their honeymoon and his eyes widened.

Polly said "Have you ever been to Disney World, Billy?"

"No, Ma'am."

"Well, next year you will, right Jim?"

Jim smiled happily. "Yes, we'll take a family vacation."

Epilogue

The keyboard player who always came for the line dancing on Friday nights began playing at 12:45 at the pavilion. They could hear the music from Polly's camper, and then at five 'til one, Polly got in Sandy's car. She had bought a new outfit for the occasion, a pink chiffon dress with pink ballet looking flats. Sandy had on a blue dress as did Brenda. When they drove up to the spot reserved for them at the lower campground, Polly could see Jim and his deputies already standing up at the front of the pavilion.

What she didn't see until the three had gotten out of the car was the police officer who had come with Jim when he came to the campground, Helen Bailey she thought was the name, seated on the back row with the lady from the detention center in Lexington. And Billy McAlpin.

Tears sprang to her eyes as he looked back at her, grinned, and stood up holding a cushion with two rings on it. He immediately walked to the front and joined Jim and the deputies. He had on a black suit, white shirt, and blue tie like the other men. Jim must have furnished it for him.

She walked up the aisle behind her two friends, with everyone she'd ever seen at the campground on both sides. The Father who led her to her new husband was her Heavenly Father, the One who had answered all the desires of her heart. No one could see Him but He was there.

When Sandy and Brenda stepped to the left, she could see Jim clearly. The love on his face almost made her trip. How blessed she was.

Lord, please take all the victims in this world and work everything out for them. Give them the love and joy you have given Jim, and Billy, and me. Thank you.

Books by Amy Barkman

Non-Fiction

Everyday Spiritual Warfare

Adult Fiction

To Love Again

Victims

A Kiss is Still a Kiss (story in collection)

Tapestry Court Series

Murder at Tapestry Court

Danger at Tapestry Court

Middle Grade Fiction

Which Witch?

Kentucky Adventures

ABOUT AMY BARKMAN

Amy Barkman has been writing professionally for many years but just recently got serious about book publication. She has written a newspaper humor column that ran for several years, radio programs, musical plays, short stories and poetry. In 2011 her first book, a non-fiction practical guide to victorious Christian living *Everyday Spiritual Warfare* was released by Next Step Books, and the first in the Fun To Be One Club midgrade series *Which Witch?* and *Murder at Tapestry Court* were released in 2012. *Kentucky Adventures* was released in 2014. *To Love Again* was released by Forget Me Not Romances in 2016. Amy has been a member of the American Association of Christian Counselors since 1989, pastor of Mortonsville United Methodist Church since 1998, and Co-Director with her husband, Gary, of Voice of Joy Ministries which she formed in 1979.

Visit Amy on the Web:
www.voiceofjoyministries.com